tell
me

OTHER BOOKS BY ABIGAIL STROM

ABIGAIL STROM

Montlake
Romance

Published by Montlake Romance, Seattle

www.apub.com

Amazon, the Amazon logo, and Montlake Romance are trademarks of Amazon.com, Inc., or its affiliates.

ISBN-13: 9781542046510
ISBN-10: 1542046513

Cover design by Damonza

Printed in the United States of America

*For Mikel, who can always find the right words
And for Owen, who went with me to Prince Edward
Island*

Chapter One

Jane Finch stopped short. She was on her way to work, but the sign in the window of one of her favorite shops had caught her eye.

Adore was a boutique that sold vintage clothing as well as modern designs. This particular display featured a blue silk dress on a mannequin, with the sign hanging above it.

Wear this and find the man of your dreams? That was some pretty bold advertising. What if you bought the dress and *didn't* meet your dream man? Would you be entitled to return it?

It was a sunny October morning: perfect weather for window-shopping in downtown Manhattan. Jane stepped out of the bustle of pedestrian traffic and gave the display a closer look.

The dress was made of soft, glossy, dark blue silk. It was tea length, with a scalloped neckline and three-quarter sleeves. The sleeves were puffed between the shoulder and the elbow, giving the dress a subtle Edwardian feel.

It was beautiful.

Beautiful and impractical. When would she ever wear something like that? She spent most of her time working in the bookstore she owned, and her last date had been three months ago. When she went out with friends, it was to the movies or a coffee shop, not to opera nights or cocktail parties.

The dress was gorgeous, but it didn't go with her lifestyle, and it was bound to be out of her price range. She might as well gaze longingly through the window at Tiffany's.

Come on, Jane. It wouldn't hurt to try it on.

That was the voice of temptation, and she almost gave in to it. But she had to open the Bookworm Turns, and on her way there, she had a novel to outline. That didn't leave time to try on beautiful clothes she'd never buy.

But as she continued down the sidewalk, it was hard to go back to the hard-boiled detective story she'd been plotting. Instead, she found herself revisiting a different kind of tale—the kind she'd told herself as a teenager.

Our heroine didn't know that today would be different. Today she would meet the man she'd convinced herself didn't exist. The hero she'd always dreamed of.

Today, she would fall in love.

She grinned to herself. Maybe she should buy the dress after all. Then she could sit down on a park bench somewhere, gaze wistfully off into the distance, and wait for romance to strike like lightning.

Caught up in her imagination, she didn't notice the crosswalk signal change until she was bumped by an irritated pedestrian.

"Oops. Sorry," she said, but the suit-clad businessman had already brushed past.

Once again keeping pace with the people around her, Jane set romance aside and returned to her thriller, murmuring the words of an opening paragraph under her breath.

"'Before the day was over, Detective Mack Connor would survive two shoot-outs, a bombing, an attempted poisoning, and—' Okay, that might be too much for the first sentence."

Mulling over other possibilities, Jane almost walked past her store.

"Jane?"

She came back to earth, blinked, and saw one of her best customers waiting at the door.

"Alicia! Have you been here long? What time is it?"

"Well . . ."

Jane pulled out her phone and checked the screen.

"Oh my gosh, it's ten fifteen. I'm so sorry. I was thinking about something on the subway and missed my stop, so I had to walk a few extra blocks. Then I got distracted by a store window." She fished her keys out of her quilted purse and unlocked the door. "You're here for the new Crochet Club mystery, right? I'll give you the loyal-customer-waiting-for-the-flaky-bookstore-owner discount."

The October breeze picked up, ruffling Alicia's short gray hair. "Nope, I'll pay full price. There's no store in this neighborhood I'd rather give my money to than yours. And you're not flaky. You're just busy having visions."

The breeze was strong enough now to tease at Jane's long brown braid, and she tucked a loose strand of hair behind her ear.

"It's sweet of you to put it like that," Jane said as she opened the door and gestured for Alicia to precede her. "I wish you could convince my family that it's visions and not flakiness that makes me late for holiday dinners."

Once inside her beloved store, Jane felt the ripple of pleasure that always went through her in the presence of books. New titles to the left, used to the right, and everywhere the scent of paper and leather bindings and the wood polish she used on the old cherry bookshelves.

"It's not sweet—it's accurate," Alicia said. "Although I will admit, I've been waiting for you to fall through an open manhole ever since I've known you. What were you thinking about that made you miss your subway stop?"

Jane went over to the windows and raised the blinds, blinking in the brilliant sunlight that streamed through the glass.

"I was plotting a thriller. A hard-boiled detective story."

"Do you think you'll actually write this one?"

Jane grinned as she went toward the cash register. "I hope so. But thinking it out is the fun part."

"With an imagination like yours, I'll never understand why you waste it on murders and mayhem. Why don't you dream up the perfect boyfriend?"

Jane went behind the counter to the shelf of special orders and customer holds. It took only a moment to find Alicia's.

"I gave that up in high school," she said, sliding the cozy mystery novel across the counter. "The gap between imagination and reality was way too depressing."

Alicia chuckled as she perused the back of the book. "I can understand that. But you're single these days, aren't you? As a single lady myself, I can tell you what I think about late at night after I've been watching Colin Firth in *Pride and Prejudice*." She glanced up from the book. "Now, if you were going to imagine the perfect man for yourself, what would he be like?"

The perfect man.

What Jane had told Alicia was true: she'd given up on the whole imaginary boyfriend thing years ago. She'd indulged her creativity plenty in high school, and the only result had been severe disappointment in real-life guys.

But now, propping her elbow on the counter and resting her chin in her hand, she remembered the sign in the shop window.

The man of your dreams.

"At least tell me what he looks like," Alicia went on, laying the book on the counter and reaching for her wallet. "You describe your ideal man, and I'll describe mine."

What would her ideal man look like these days? Now that she was twenty-seven and not seventeen?

"Dark-haired," she said, straightening up and running Alicia's credit card. "The best heroes are always dark-haired."

"Eyes?"

"Gray. A steely gray that belies his kind heart. A handsome, rugged face, saved from being too perfect by a nose that has been broken at least once—doing something heroic, of course. Getting into a bar fight to defend a woman's honor, rescuing a kidnapped toddler, rushing into the street to save a dog from being run over. That sort of thing." She handed Alicia her receipt. "But he's intelligent, too. And he loves to read. Manly stuff like Twain and Kipling, but he'll be open to Jane Austen after I tell him how awesome she is."

"Mmmm, perfect. I'm in love already."

Jane slid Alicia's purchase into a plastic bag. "Okay, now you. Colin Firth, I presume?"

Alicia's eyes widened as she caught sight of something through the store window. "I was about to say yes, but I've just been reminded that there's one type of hero I like even better than Mr. Darcy."

Jane turned her head, but a bookcase blocked her line of sight. "What type?"

"Cowboy. Oh my goodness, I think he's coming in here."

A cowboy in Manhattan? Coming into her bookstore?

A little tingle ran down her spine. Could it be—?

No, Caleb and her sister were still away. Weren't they? But then who—

The bell chimed as the door opened.

It *was* him. Caleb Bryce.

He paused for a moment inside the door, letting his eyes adjust after the bright October sunlight outside. Then he came toward the register where Jane and Alicia were standing, both women watching his approach.

His face was shadowed by his old brown felt cowboy hat, but Jane could see his mouth—and the familiar half grin that tipped up one corner.

It was easier to imagine Caleb riding a horse than strolling through a Manhattan bookstore. Since he'd grown up on a Colorado ranch and owned a company that led wilderness treks around the world, that made a certain amount of sense.

It had been a month since Jane had last seen Caleb, right before he and Samantha had left for a trip to the Canadian Rockies. Jane hadn't realized they were back.

Caleb Bryce was many things. A wilderness expert, her sister's business partner, and an old friend who was like a brother to her.

But there was one thing he most definitely was *not*.

Jane's ideal man.

Her ideal man wouldn't tease her for being a bookworm who didn't play sports or go camping. Her ideal man wouldn't criticize her for living in her imagination, as he put it, and caring more about dreams than reality. Her ideal man wouldn't badger her to go with him and Samantha on one of their hiking expeditions when he knew she was afraid of heights, bears, spiders, landslides, getting lost in the woods, and dying of cold and exposure on a mountainside.

Even in the looks department Caleb didn't quite fit the bill. His hair was light brown, not dark, and his eyes were a muddy and uninspiring hazel.

Okay, so those eyes *did* have a lot of humor and intelligence behind them . . . but they turned mocking and derisive much too often. And yes, his face *was* handsome . . . but his nose had never been broken. That, along with the cleft in his chin, made his features a little too perfect.

It was harder to find fault with his body. He was tall and strong and powerful, which definitely made for hero material.

Not that she was noticing. Caleb was the big brother she'd never had, and thoughts about his body were out-of-bounds.

It would help if his clothes didn't draw attention to his lean, powerful musculature. His jeans, old and worn, hung low on his narrow hips. His denim shirt, also worn, stretched tight across his broad shoulders.

Everything about him screamed testosterone.

Too much testosterone for her ideal man. Her hero would be masculine, of course . . . but he would also be sensitive. A bookworm, like her. Not a man who scoffed at the very idea of reading, like Caleb. And he—

Caleb stopped next to Alicia, returning the older woman's smile before turning to Jane. When she didn't say anything right away, he reached across the counter and tugged at her braid.

"Hey there, darlin'," he said. "Aren't you going to say hello?"

The brush of Caleb's fingers made heat crawl up the back of her neck.

"Hello," she said almost grudgingly, knowing she didn't sound particularly happy to see him. Better that than sounding *too* happy, though. Caleb didn't need any help in the ego department.

"Well, I guess I'll go home and read my new book," Alicia said, her expression telling Jane she could expect a quiz about Caleb the next time she came in. "But before I go, young man, I don't suppose you'd care to do a favor for an old woman?"

Caleb grinned at her. "I will if I can find one. I only see young ladies in here."

"Very gallant," Alicia said, smiling up at him.

Caleb cocked his head to the side. "What's the favor, ma'am?"

Her smile widened. "That was it. I wanted to hear you call me *ma'am*. Ideally while tipping your hat, but that'll do."

Caleb chuckled, and then he moved to get ahead of Alicia as she headed for the door. He pulled it open and held it for her, and as she passed him, he tipped his hat. "Have a good day, ma'am."

Jane shook her head at him as he came back toward her.

"Charming my customers? Really?"

"I'll always do a favor for a lady," he said, reaching out to tug her braid again. "Even you, pipsqueak."

She hated that nickname. Among other things, it reminded her that Samantha was the statuesque, beautiful older sister while she'd been dubbed Plain Jane by Sam's first boyfriend.

"Don't do that," she said, wishing she didn't sound like an easily goaded little sister.

"Do what? This?"

Caleb tugged at her hair again before taking a step back and appraising her lazily. "You know, you *are* a grown-ass woman. Maybe it's time to lose the braid."

"I don't need grooming advice from you, thanks all the same. But while we're on the subject, you know this is New York City, right? We're not out on the prairie. You don't have to dress like an ad for cowboy cologne."

Caleb swept off his hat and bowed, and her lips twitched in spite of herself.

His teasing could definitely be annoying. But as he straightened up and grinned at her, she knew a part of her enjoyed their verbal sparring.

"Whatever you say, ma'am." He tossed the hat toward the shelf behind her, and of course it landed perfectly. "Now, may I ask for some assistance? You've got a paying customer here."

A lock of his too-long brown hair fell across his forehead. Without his hat shadowing them, his hazel eyes seemed greener, especially against his tanned and weather-toughened skin.

She focused on his words. "You, a customer? Since when do you buy books?"

"Since your sister's got a birthday coming up."

Jane raised an eyebrow. "Sam's birthday isn't for two weeks. I think you've got time. Also, she doesn't read."

"Yeah, but you do."

She looked at Caleb suspiciously. "How is that relevant?"

"You'll see. Now point me toward your travel section, please."

◆　◆　◆

Caleb grinned to himself as he followed Jane through the labyrinth of bookcases. He was determined, this time, to succeed in his years-long effort to get Jane's nose out of her books and her head out of the clouds, and to get her away from the city and into the great outdoors. He hadn't yet come close to accomplishing that goal, but persistence was his middle name.

Caleb had a brother but no sisters—at least, not until he'd met Jane and Samantha Finch.

Samantha was like his twin. They had the same interests and skills, and they meshed perfectly as business partners. Jane, on the other hand, was the kid sister he had nothing in common with, the one he loved to tease, the one who—

His thoughts stuttered to a halt.

Jane had knocked a book from a table display as she brushed past it, and now she was bending over to pick it up.

In the instant before he forced himself to look away, that image of Jane was burned into his brain. Her curving hips. The bare skin of her lower back when her navy-blue shirt rode up. The incurve of her spine, creating a dimple above the waistband of her jeans. Her perfect butt.

"Caleb?"

Get it together.

He took a deep breath and focused on Jane again.

They were near one of the store windows, and a shaft of sunlight picked out strands of gold in her brown hair. Her skin glowed. When she blinked, the shadows of her long lashes were visible on her cheek-bones, behind the lenses of her tortoiseshell glasses.

"Caleb?" she asked again, frowning a little.

"What?" he asked, his voice harsher than he'd intended. What the hell had she said, anyway?

"I said, here's the travel section. Now tell me. How is the fact that I read relevant to my sister's birthday?"

Samantha's birthday. Right.

He cleared his throat. "You'll see." He gestured toward the door, where two women were just coming in. "Go ahead and help your other customers. I know what I'm looking for."

By the time he found the titles he wanted, he was feeling back to normal. Jane was and would always be a friend to him. Period.

There were several customers in the store now, but they were all browsing and no one was at the register. He strolled over to Jane and laid his two selections on the counter.

"I'll take these, Madame Bookseller."

Jane looked down at the two titles. "*The Appalachian Trail in New York*? Maybe. But *The Beginner's Guide to Backpacking*? That's the worst birthday present ever. Samantha's not a beginner. She knows more than you do."

He grinned at her. "You'll never get me to admit that. And anyway, the book's not for Sam. It's for you."

Jane's eyes widened. Then, after a moment, they narrowed.

"No way. If you're trying to lure me out into the hinterlands, you can just—"

Caleb rested his forearms on the counter and leaned toward her. "Come on," he said. "Sam's only going to turn thirty once. You know there's no present she'd love more than a hiking trip for the three of us. Just a few days, maybe a week. Not Mount Everest or the Alps or the Rockies. All we have to do is drive north for an hour and a half, and we'll hit the Appalachian Trail. We won't even have to leave the state."

She started to answer, but then her eyes shifted to someone behind him.

"I haven't finished browsing yet," a male voice said, "but may I leave these here while I do?"

"Of course," Jane said after a moment. She sounded almost startled, and Caleb turned to get a look at the customer.

He was too late. All he saw was the man's back as he disappeared into the maze of books.

He turned back to Jane. "On my honor, I promise to protect you from spiders, bears, and avalanches."

Jane was focused on him again. Her eyes were big and dark blue, and her long lashes made them seem even bigger. "How would you protect me from an avalanche? You can't stop an avalanche."

"There won't be one, so it won't come up."

"How do you know there won't be one?"

"Because an avalanche is the rapid flow of snow and ice down a sloping surface. There won't be any snow when we go."

"Hmm."

Caleb loved to argue with Jane. It was one of his favorite things to do when he came to the city between wilderness trips, because he could always needle her into a response. Now, though, she seemed a little distracted. When she looked at something over his shoulder for the third time, he turned his head.

It was the man who'd come up behind him a moment ago. He was standing about twenty feet away, gazing at the book in his hand the way Caleb looked at a rib-eye steak.

"What's up with that guy? You keep staring at him." Caleb leaned toward Jane and lowered his voice a little. "Think he's a shoplifter?"

"Don't be silly." She hesitated. "He just reminds me of someone I was thinking about this morning."

"Reminds you of someone? Who?"

Jane took a deep breath and let it out slowly.

"My ideal man."

Chapter Two

Caleb's spine stiffened, as though he were a dog or a wolf getting ready to fight.

He ignored the sensation and gave the customer another glance.

"That guy? You're not serious. He's wearing glasses."

Jane glared at him. "What are you, twelve? Grown-ups don't criticize people for wearing glasses." She folded her arms. "And in case you've forgotten, *I* wear glasses."

Caleb held up his hands. "Hey, whatever. I'm just saying most women don't think men in glasses are sexy."

"There's so much wrong with that sentence I don't even know where to start. For one thing, I'm not most women. For another, smart is the new sexy. Or hadn't you heard?"

He grinned at her. "If you say so. But at least I don't—"

She smacked him again. "Shh! He's coming."

Back in high school and college, Caleb was the guy girls shushed each other over when he came near. He'd tried not to get a swelled head over it, but the fact was, he'd never had a problem getting women to notice him.

Of course, he wasn't interested in Jane romantically. The resentment he felt toward Mr. Ideal Man was just on general principle. Because if *any* woman found this guy more desirable than, say, him, the world no longer made sense.

The man had short dark hair, sideburns, and a goatee. A freaking *goatee.* He was tall, and while he had a decent build, it was the kind of build you got in a gym as opposed to actually playing a sport or working outdoors. Between the professorial-looking tweed jacket and the horn-rims, Caleb guessed he spent most of his time reading.

Just like Jane.

Horn-Rims came to a stop across from her and smiled, and Jane smiled back.

And with that one smile, it felt like a heavy stone settled in the pit of his stomach.

Caleb had been judging—and dismissing—this dude as an elitist hipster nerd without any evidence other than his physical appearance and the fact that he was in a bookstore. Then he'd gone a step further in his head, deciding he couldn't be Jane's ideal man because . . . opposites should attract? Or something.

But now that he saw the two of them smiling at each other, he imagined what Sam would say if she were here.

Oh my God, they look so cute together!

And as much as he hated to admit it, it was true.

Between Jane's glasses and the guy's horn-rims, the two of them were blinking owlishly at each other like lovebirds in a bookworm's paradise.

It wasn't just the glasses. There was something alike in the shy smiles they gave each other. Then the guy asked a question about the book he was holding, and Jane answered, and there was something alike in the way they spoke, too. They sounded eager, interested, enthusiastic.

The way he sounded talking about camping equipment with other hikers, or horses with his brother.

So maybe opposites didn't attract. Maybe the more obvious conclusion was true: people were attracted to each other when they had something in common.

Attracted.

The word was like another stone in his gut.

Because that was what he was seeing. Attraction.

There was a pink glow in Jane's cheeks that hadn't been there before. She rested her arms on the counter as she leaned toward the man, as though wanting to get closer. They were talking about the cover illustration, and when they reached for the book at the same time, their hands touched.

The blush in Jane's cheeks deepened as she jerked her hand back, ducking her head for a moment before looking up again.

When Caleb realized that his own hands had fisted and his jaw had hardened into granite, he forced himself to relax.

He focused on the book they were so interested in and spoke abruptly.

"*A Little Princess.* That's a kids' book, right? Do you have kids? Are you married?"

Jane whipped her head around to glare at him before turning back to her customer.

"Please forgive my friend for that personal question. He was raised in a barn. Literally. Also, if you'll give me a moment to ring him up, he was just leaving. Then I can show you the rare books section I was talking about. I have a first edition of *The Secret Garden* I think you'll love."

He was being dismissed, which pissed him off.

"I'm a little more than a friend," Caleb said as he pulled out his wallet.

"That's true," Jane agreed as she ran his card and slid his books into a bag. "He's my sister's business partner, which makes him my honorary big brother. I've often wondered if an actual big brother would be half as annoying."

That pissed him off, too, in spite of the fact that he'd called himself Jane's honorary big brother a hundred times.

"Yeah, well—"

She slid the bag across the counter toward him. "Thank you, sir, and do please come again."

Damn it, he hadn't even gotten to the other reason he'd stopped by. He was supposed to make dinner plans for the three of them.

"Sam and I—"

"Want to get together now that you're back in the city. Sure. I'll call Sam tonight to figure out where and when, okay?"

Jane and Sam would figure out dinner, he'd paid for his books, and Jane had made it crystal clear it was time for him to go.

He glanced over at Mr. Ideal Man, who was looking at Jane. He was probably ready for Caleb to leave, too.

He slid the bag back toward Jane. "These are for you, remember? To persuade you to go hiking for Sam's birthday."

She stuck the books under the counter. "The answer is no way, but we can talk about that later. Bye, Caleb."

He was running out of excuses to stay.

He nodded toward the hat he'd tossed onto the shelf behind her. "My hat, if you please."

She grabbed it and handed it to him.

"Thank you, ma'am," he said as he put it on, but her attention wasn't on him anymore. She was looking at Horn-Rims with an expression that made him want to hit something . . . or someone.

Caleb exited the store into the bright sunlight, tipping the brim of his Stetson down to shade his eyes. As he strolled down the sidewalk, he tried to recapture the feeling of happiness and anticipation he'd felt just an hour before. He'd thought at the time that the feeling came from the beautiful October day, his enjoyment of the city he hadn't seen in a month, and the prospect of seeing Jane and planning something fun for Sam's birthday.

He was still in the city, the sun was still shining, and he hadn't given up hope for a family hiking trip.

But his pleasure in those things was gone.

◆　◆　◆

Jane was still mad at Caleb for his big-brother-ish intrusion, but as soon as he left, it occurred to her that his too-personal question *did* give her an opportunity for a (hopefully less awkward) follow-up.

"So," she said, hoping she sounded casual as she led the handsome stranger toward the rare books she kept in a locked glass cabinet. "Since you're interested in children's books, I'm assuming you're looking for a gift? We offer free wrapping if you are," she added quickly, going for professional as well as casual.

"I need a present for my eight-year-old niece," he said, which, along with the bare ring finger on his left hand, was music to her ears.

Take that, Caleb Bryce. He's single.

"I loved *The Secret Garden* when I was eight," she said, unlocking the glass doors of the rare books case and pausing to breathe in her favorite scent—the faint musty sweetness of leather bindings and old paper. "Then there's *Little Women*, or *The Lion, the Witch, and the Wardrobe*. I've also got a beautiful edition of *Anne of Green Gables*."

He raised his eyebrows. "*Anne of Green Gables*? I used to read that one to my sister."

She felt a rush of pleasure. "You did? That's one of my all-time favorites."

"It was my sister's favorite, too. I practically had it memorized by the time she turned ten."

He'd read to his sister when they were kids? That was adorable.

Now for the really important question.

"Did you like it?"

She almost held her breath waiting for the answer.

"Actually, I loved it. I never told Lisa that, of course."

That was said with a self-deprecating grin that would have convinced Jane—as if she'd needed any convincing—that this man was meant for her.

As if to prove that the universe agreed with her, her employee Felicia came in to work an hour early, freeing Jane up to give Tall, Dark, and Handsome her undivided attention.

By the time he finally got around to buying something, they'd talked books and their favorite authors for more than an hour. They'd exchanged first names—his was Dan, which became Handsome Dan in her mind almost immediately—and Jane had managed to mention (casually, please God) that she was single.

The only negative was that Dan hadn't found an opportunity to say he was single, too, even though she was almost positive he was. Also on the con side, he hadn't given her a business card or his phone number or suggested they get together for coffee or lunch or dinner.

He paid for his illustrated copy of *Alice in Wonderland* in cash, which was a little disappointing. A credit card would have showed his last name. But then, as she was taking way too much time to wrap his niece's gift and trying to think of a way to prolong their interaction, he said, "Is there any chance you might be working tomorrow afternoon?"

Stay calm. Don't answer too fast, and don't jump up and down.

She slipped the wrapped book into a bag and set it on the counter.

"Yes, I'm working until closing time tomorrow. Six o'clock."

Warm and friendly but not overly enthusiastic. *Good girl, Jane.*

He took the bag and smiled at her. "I might drop by with my niece around four o'clock. I think she'd love this place, and then she can pick out a book of her own to go with the one I chose for her."

"That would be great!" *Too much.* "I mean, I always love an excuse to talk about my favorite children's books. Bring her by anytime." *Better.*

He smiled at her again. "Until we meet again."

That was nice. Sort of old-fashioned and formal.

"You bet."

She winced. *You bet?* Was that the best she could come up with?

It was too late to think of something better, though. He was already gone, the door closing behind him.

◆ ◆ ◆

Handsome Dan.

Jane finished the rest of the day in a glow, trying to tell herself he might not come back after all but not really believing it because he had to have felt the same connection she had. Didn't he?

By the time she was back in Brooklyn, climbing the stairs to her third-floor apartment, she was feeling a lot less certain. After all, statistically speaking, it must be a hundred times easier to meet a single female bookworm in Manhattan than a single male bookworm. In other words, there were a lot more Plain Janes in the city than Handsome Dans.

Maybe he wasn't single. He didn't wear a wedding ring, but he might be dating someone.

See "statistically speaking," above.

By the time she was in bed with her current book—a biography of Eleanor Roosevelt—she'd gone from happy glow to Gloomy Gus. She was positive now that she would never see Handsome Dan again. And not only had she acted like a giddy schoolgirl around a total stranger, but she'd made a fool of herself in front of Caleb Bryce.

If only Caleb hadn't been there, she could consign the incident to oblivion and never think of it again. But he'd be sure to ask her about the customer she'd called her "ideal man," and the only thing she wanted to be able to tell him was that he'd asked her out on a date.

Sigh.

She set her book on the nightstand, turned off the light, and curled up on her side to go to sleep.

But sleep didn't come. She replayed the events of the day, and when she was done, one question stood out.

Why had she gotten so excited about some random customer? Was she that hard up for a little romance in her life?

Her sister—who never had trouble getting a guy to ask her out—would say yes. And Caleb, who always told her she was too shy and cautious about relationships (and everything else), would say yes, too.

She shifted in bed, turning on her other side to face the window. It was open, and the crisp, fall-scented breeze teased through her bedroom, raising the fine hairs on her forearms and making her burrow a little deeper into the blankets.

The contrast of cool air and warm covers made her extra-aware of her body. How long had it been since she'd shared her bed with a man?

Too damn long, apparently.

Giving up on the idea of falling into a peaceful slumber, she sat up in bed and rested her chin on her knees, staring out at the full moon.

It really was a beautiful night. The wind picked up, tossing the tree branches outside her window, and the rustling leaves sounded like ocean waves.

Autumn always made her feel restless.

Maybe that's all this was. A sort of seasonal discontent with her life, which was, no denying it, a little quiet lately. Maybe she'd gotten excited about Handsome Dan because he represented the possibility of something new, a kind of adventure. Caleb was always telling her she needed more adventure in her life.

Damn Caleb anyway. Why did he keep popping up in her thoughts?

Her thoughts were her own, and it bugged her that Caleb had the power to interrupt them. Her mind was the one place where she was all-powerful. She'd always reveled in her imagination, using it to conjure up dragons and unicorns and fantasy realms, plots of global conspiracy and assassination . . . and yes, the occasional dream man.

But it had been a while since she'd conjured up an imaginary lover to keep her company on a lonely night.

Maybe it was time to change that, at least.

She settled back down into her pillows, drawing the covers up to her chin and thinking of Handsome Dan. His dark hair and blue eyes, his charmingly bookish glasses, his cowboy hat . . .

Wait a minute. His cowboy hat? Where the heck had that come from?

She started over again. Handsome Dan was talking with her about Charles Dickens and Jules Verne, only this time he asked her out for a drink so they could continue their conversation.

What would they have? Red wine, local beer, artisanal cocktails?

Kentucky bourbon, pipsqueak. Neat. No chaser.

Grrrrr.

Okay, maybe she should cut right to the good stuff. Caleb wouldn't show up during the hot part because he was a friend. An honorary brother. And rule number one about friends and honorary brothers was that you didn't picture them naked.

Handsome Dan was here in her bedroom. He was taking off his clothes, his eyes on her the whole time, and—

Her phone vibrated on the nightstand, ruining the moment.

She jerked upright and grabbed it, glaring at the screen. Who would be calling this late?

Caleb. Of course.

The bastard had managed to interrupt the naked part of her fantasy, too.

She hit Accept.

"What."

"That's how you answer the phone?"

He sounded amused, which was irritating.

"Only when it's you, and only when I'm in bed."

"You're in bed, huh? And you answered my call. I guess that means you're alone. If not, Horn-Rims must be pissed right now."

She gritted her teeth. Then she took a deep breath and counted to ten.

"Very funny. Why are you calling, Caleb?"

"You said you'd talk to Sam about dinner, but she says she didn't hear from you."

It was true; she'd forgotten to call Sam. But, still—

"That's not a good enough reason to call this late. And you guys are in the city for a few weeks, right? Before your next trip? That's plenty of time for the three of us to get together. What's the rush?"

There was a short silence.

"No rush," he said after a moment. "But when Sam mentioned you hadn't called her, it occurred to me that you might have been, uh, distracted. By Horn-Rims."

Caleb had already found an insulting nickname for him. Great.

"His name is Dan."

Another short silence.

"So, you're on a first-name basis? Fast work, pipsqueak. I didn't know you had it in you."

"You're impressed that I found out his name? A minute ago you wondered if he was in bed with me."

"That was a joke. Truth is, I figured things with Horn-Rims would stay where your real-life opportunities always do."

She was going to regret asking this question, but she could never leave well enough alone when it came to Caleb.

"And where's that?"

"In your head."

She was lying flat on her back, staring up at the ceiling. There was a water stain she kept meaning to paint over that looked sort of like a male profile, and it was easy enough to imagine it was Caleb's.

She stuck her tongue out at it. "And what's *that* supposed to mean?"

"You never go after what you want. You think about things, but you don't do them. You have this big imagination, but your reality is . . ."

He trailed off without finishing.

"What? My reality is what?"

Boring. He was going to say *boring*.

"Not everything it could be," he said after a moment.

Okay, that was more diplomatic than she'd expected. But even so—

"You're only saying that because I don't climb mountains or BASE jump or go over waterfalls in a barrel."

"I've never gone over a waterfall in a barrel."

"But not everyone wants to do those things. I like my life, even if you think it's boring."

"I didn't say your life was boring," he said quickly, which probably meant that was exactly what he thought.

She didn't agree, but she also knew she'd never convince him otherwise. Because what she found thrilling was exactly what he dismissed as unimportant.

Caleb Bryce was a doer. An adventurer. A man of action. To him, only what you could see and touch and taste was real. How could she ever explain to him that her thoughts and dreams were as real to her as the physical world? That her imagination was as precious to her as anything in his life was to him?

She couldn't, of course.

"This conversation is pointless," she said after a moment. "We're too different. We'll never agree on what makes an interesting life. Or anything else, probably. So I guess it's a good thing you're always jumping out of an airplane or scaling a mountaintop, and I don't have to see you that much."

Another silence. This one went on long enough that she checked her phone screen to make sure the call hadn't disconnected.

"Caleb? Are you there?"

"Yeah," he said. "I'm here."

Chapter Three

He didn't know why her words bugged him so much. One of the benefits of teasing the people you cared about was not taking any of it seriously. God knew he didn't hold back when he was teasing her.

But this time, the line between teasing and touching a nerve had gotten a little hazy.

"Caleb?"

"I'm here," he said again.

Unlike Jane, he wasn't in bed. He was in the living room of his Washington Heights apartment, his home base between expeditions—which meant it was a place he didn't see very often.

His aunt Rosemary had wanted his home base to be in Colorado, near his childhood home, but that was the last place he would have picked. He loved his aunt, but even she couldn't get him back to the ranch more than once or twice a year.

When his brother was picked for NASA's astronaut candidate program, he'd tried to convince Caleb to make his home base in Houston. Caleb would have been okay with that, but Sam had pointed out (rightly enough) that they didn't know how long Hunter would be in Texas once the training program was over. She'd wanted their headquarters to be in New York City, where she and Jane had grown up and where Jane had returned after inheriting her grandparents' bookstore. She was also willing to consider LA, where they'd moved when they were teenagers and where their parents still lived.

Sam had left the final choice to him, and he'd gone with New York.

"Your parents have each other, but Jane's on her own," he'd said to Sam.

"We'll be away at least half the time. It's not like she'll be able to count on us being there."

"Sure, but she still needs us more than your folks do."

"You better not tell Jane that. She hates the idea of anyone trying to take care of her."

"She hates it when *you* try to take care of her," Caleb had corrected. "I'm more subtle about it, so she doesn't notice as much."

"You're not subtle. And I thought you hated New York."

"I'd hate living there all the time. But it's not a bad place to visit, and I know how much you love it. That's a good enough reason to make it our home base."

Sam had a studio in the East Village, and he'd found a one-bedroom he liked in Washington Heights. If money was tight, they could sublet their places when they were on expeditions, but when business was good he preferred to leave his empty. He always scoffed at the idea of settling down anywhere, but the truth was, a part of him liked the idea of having a place somewhere that was his, waiting for him to come home to.

He was there now, sitting in a leather chair by the window, staring at the moon above the Manhattan skyline.

"It's almost midnight," Jane was saying. "I'll call Sam tomorrow, okay? We'll figure out dinner then. There's plenty of time."

She was going to hang up. It was late, and she probably wanted to get to sleep.

But he was wide awake and as restless now as he'd been before he'd called her. He wasn't ready to say good night.

"So did Horn-Rims ask you out, or what?"

"Dan. His name is Dan."

If that's what it took to keep her talking.

"Fine, whatever. Did *Dan* ask you out?"

A short silence. Then: "No. But he's coming by the store tomorrow."

There was a small tug in his stomach, like someone had pulled a rope knot a little tighter.

"Yeah? Good for you. Did you give him your digits?"

"I just met him *today*. Why would I give him my phone number?"

"Are you serious? Damn, Jane, you're worse off than I thought. How do you think relationships start?"

"Meeting someone. Talking to them. Finding out you have things in common. And—"

"They start by giving a guy your phone number."

"It's too soon for that. I think it's better to talk in person first."

"But if you have someone's phone number, you can have late-night flirting calls."

"Late-night flirting calls?"

"Don't tell me you've never done that."

"Well, I haven't. I mean, I've dated, obviously, and spoken to boyfriends on the phone—"

"What are you wearing?"

"What?"

"I said, what are you wearing?"

"Right now? Pajamas. Why are you—"

"Jane. You don't say pajamas."

"What are you talking about?"

She sounded genuinely bewildered. What the hell was he doing, anyway?

"If a guy asks you what you're wearing when he calls you at bedtime, you say nothing."

"I don't say anything?"

Jesus.

"No. You say *nothing*. As in, you're *wearing* nothing. As in, you're naked." He paused. "Okay, let's try this again. What are you wearing?"

Silence. Then: "Oh my God, Caleb. This is nuts on so many levels."

She wasn't wrong about that.

"I'm just trying to—"

"First of all, I *am* wearing pajamas. I always wear pajamas. To bed, that is. And second of all, you're not a guy." She paused. "I mean . . . damn it, you know what I mean."

Yeah, he did. But it didn't feel great to hear her say it, which was also nuts on many levels.

"I was just giving you a chance to practice."

"To practice *what?*"

"Late-night flirting calls. In case you want to make something happen with Dan instead of just thinking about it."

"You make it sound like I've never dated anyone before. But you know I have. I—"

"How long has it been?"

Silence.

How long *had* it been, anyway? Since he'd heard Jane talk about a guy?

"I went on a date three months ago," she said after a moment, sounding defensive.

"A date, singular? What happened?"

"We didn't go on another one. Obviously."

The phone felt warm in his hand, as though it were working harder to get a signal. Caleb shifted in his chair, stretching his legs out in front of him and hooking one ankle over the other.

"Why not?"

He could almost hear her shrug over the phone. She shrugged a lot—when she was annoyed, when she was uncomfortable, when she was feeling shy.

"I don't know. No chemistry, I guess."

"For you, or for him?"

"For both of us. What's with the inquisition, anyway? Why do you care how my last date went?"

Good question.

"I'm just trying to help you out here, pipsqueak. You seemed pretty excited about ol' Dan today, and I'd hate to see you screw it up."

"Thank you so much," she said drily. "That's very encouraging."

His head was tilted as he relaxed back in the chair, and now he smiled up at the ceiling. "So go ahead and practice on me."

"Practice . . ."

"Your late-night phone flirting skills. They might lead you to a second date someday."

"Even if I accepted your premise that I'm bad at flirting, which I don't, I wouldn't practice on you."

He could almost feel her glaring at him. "Why not?"

"Because it would be embarrassing, you moron."

"But I'm not a guy. You said so yourself. Go ahead, Jane, let me hear you flirt. What are you wearing?"

"Pajamas."

He smiled again. "Okay, fine, we'll go with that. What kind of pajamas?"

An audible sigh. "Harry Potter pajamas."

He blinked. "You can't be serious."

"Of course I'm serious."

"Wow. Okay, you really are worse off than I thought."

"You know, Mr. Smug Pants, there's every chance that a fellow Harry Potter geek would find them adorable."

Mr. Smug Pants. That was pretty funny.

"Does that mean your dating pool is limited to fellow Harry Potter geeks?"

"Why not? Your dating pool is limited to Amazonian athletes with buns of steel and big tits."

He sat up a little straighter. "Hey! That's not true."

"I'm quoting Sam. That's what she said about you the last time you guys were in town."

"I see. And what did she base *that* conclusion on?"

"I'm thinking she based it on reality. We were at a bar at the time, and Sam and I were watching you hit on an Amazonian athlete with buns of steel and big tits."

Damn. Who in the hell—?

Oh, right. Rita.

"Fine. Even assuming you and your sister have a point, *tits* is a demeaning word. I prefer breasts."

"Wow. You're a true feminist hero, Caleb."

"I know. That's one of the many reasons chicks dig me."

"Okay, I'm going to bed. In my Harry Potter pajamas. Ravenclaw house colors, if you're interested."

"I don't know what that means."

"You've never read the Harry Potter books?"

She sounded more horrified by that than by anything else he'd said.

Had he read them? "In elementary school, maybe."

"But you don't remember them? See, this is why we'd never be friends if it wasn't for Sam. Those books were my whole life for a couple of years."

"Geek."

"Jock."

"Four-eyes."

"Muscle-head."

He was grinning now, picturing Jane sitting up in bed as they traded insults. Her long brown hair would be down, and she wouldn't be wearing her glasses.

"Hey, Jane? Take a selfie and send it to me."

"So you can make fun of my pajamas?"

"Nope. So I can see what Ravenclaw house colors look like. I don't want to be an ignorant muscle-head, after all."

He heard her chuckle. "I don't think one selfie will help with that, but okay. I'm hanging up now, and then I'll send it." A short pause. "Good night, Caleb."

"Good night, Jane."

Silence settled over his apartment after the call ended. Outside, the moon had risen a little higher. Earlier there had been ragged clouds chasing across it, blown fast by the October wind, but now it shone clear and bright. He stared at it, thinking of the night skies he'd seen on the Big Island of Hawaii and the slopes of Mount Kilimanjaro.

Places Jane would never go with him.

His phone buzzed, and he looked at the picture she'd sent.

She was sitting up in bed, cross-legged, her back against the pillows. Her sheets were white, and her comforter was pale blue. Her bedside lamp had one of those stained-glass lampshades. What were they called? Tiffany.

But the only thing in the picture he really focused on was Jane.

Her hair *was* down, like he'd imagined. He'd seen it down before, but he'd forgotten how long and thick and satiny it was and how the word *brown* really couldn't do it justice. Because there were a thousand colors in there, threads of bronze and gold and red, like leaves in mid-November.

His hand tightened on the phone.

Without her glasses, her eyes were big pools of dark blue, as deep as the ocean. And he had proof that she didn't use mascara or anything to make her eyelashes so long and thick, because she wasn't wearing any makeup now and there they were.

There *she* was.

His honorary kid sister.

A sudden rush of guilt made him switch off the phone, and he levered himself up and out of the chair. It was time for him to go to bed, too.

But even with the phone off he could still see Jane, her cheeks pink and her skin glowing, her soft lips curving up in a smile and those dark blue eyes gazing into the camera.

Chapter Four

Jane and Sam worked out their dinner plans via text the next morning.

Sam: How about the place around the corner from your store? The one where they do the fancy hamburgers and have all that Star Trek stuff on the walls?

Jane: Caleb hates that place. He thinks it's pretentious.

Sam: He thinks everything is pretentious. We haven't started caring about that, have we?

Jane: Good point. Kobe-yashi Maru it is. 7?

Sam: 7

Jane slid her phone back into her pocket and went back to what was really important: deciding what top to wear for her second meeting with Handsome Dan.

She'd already decided on her favorite jeans because they made her butt look good. But her butt always looked pretty good, while the same couldn't be said for her top half. She'd teased Caleb about preferring women with big breasts, but the fact was, most men did. She'd read somewhere that it was biological—big breasts signaled that a woman was fertile and able to nourish a baby, so men were hardwired to be attracted to that.

Which meant they weren't hardwired to be attracted to her.

But she did own one padded bra, and it ratcheted her up from an A/B to a B/C and gave her something approaching cleavage. Pair that with the right top and she'd be in business.

She decided to go with a bookworm T-shirt—the one with a zombie librarian saying BOOKS . . . BOOKS . . . BOOKS instead of BRAINS . . . BRAINS . . . BRAINS.

There were three good reasons for her choice: wearing a T-shirt meant you weren't trying too hard; this particular T-shirt had a V-neck that would accentuate her artificial cleavage; and it was funny. Not to people like Caleb, maybe, but to people like her and Dan.

She usually needed only one employee to close with her, but she'd asked Kiki to double up with Felicia today so she'd be able to focus on Dan even if there was a rush of customers . . . which, as a small business owner, she supposed she ought to be hoping for.

But to be honest, on this particular day, what she was really hoping for was to see Dan again.

And that this time, he'd ask her on a date.

On the subway from Brooklyn to downtown Manhattan, she found herself thinking about last night's conversation with Caleb. Remembering it sent odd sensations running through her, little ripples of . . . something.

Was he right about her flirting abilities—or rather, her lack of them? It was true she didn't do a lot of flirting with guys she was interested in . . . she was usually more focused on finding shared interests and in trying to have a real conversation.

A wave of depression made her slump down on the plastic seat. Across from her, a young woman—a student, judging by the backpack—was angry-texting on her smartphone, glaring at the screen like it was the boyfriend Jane was certain she was fighting with.

Relationships suck, Sam always said. *People mistake lust for love, and then things get messy.*

Maybe Caleb was right and she was wrong. Maybe guys didn't care about shared interests. Maybe they cared about late-night flirting calls and big breasts.

Maybe Sam was right, and love would always take a back seat to lust.

But a few hours later, when she was surrounded by books and customers who loved them, her native optimism returned. Of course there were men in the world looking for real relationships. And some of those men were guy-nerds, men who watched *Doctor Who* and loved Harry Potter and could say at least a few words in J. R. R. Tolkien's elvish language. Men who saw geekdom and a love of literature not as an impediment, but as the perfect bridge to romance.

By the time four o'clock rolled around, she was feeling downright cheery.

She didn't even have time to doubt herself, to wonder if maybe Dan wouldn't come. Because at 4:05 there he was, bringing not only his niece but his sister. And when he spotted her he came right over, smiling like they'd known each other for years and introducing Lisa (his sister) and Alice (his niece) as though he'd already told them about Jane and had been looking forward to seeing her all day.

The four of them chatted about books and authors, and Alice picked out an autographed copy of E. B. White's *Charlotte's Web* from the rare-books case.

Jane's one niggling concern was how she and Dan would get down to the date question—or at least the phone number question—with his sister and niece there. But before she had a chance to come up with a potential solution, Dan found one himself.

Or rather, his niece did.

"Come on, Mom, we're going to be late," she said, tugging on Lisa's arm.

Lisa pulled out her phone and nodded. "You're right, we are." She smiled at Jane. "It's your fault for being so charming. It was lovely to meet you, and we'll be sure to come here for our Christmas shopping. Dan, will we see you soon?"

He nodded. "Not tonight, though."

Jane's hopes soared as Lisa and Alice left. What was he planning to do tonight? Could it be something he wanted to do with her? Dinner? Dancing? Drinks? All three? Of course she was wearing a T-shirt while he was wearing a maroon button-down over gray wool slacks, but she always kept a few pieces of clothing here at the store. She had a skirt hanging up in the back room should it become necessary.

Please let it become necessary.

Dan started to say something and then stopped. He fiddled with his glasses, which made her think about how often she fiddled with her own glasses when she was nervous.

Was he nervous? About asking her out, maybe?

After a moment he took the glasses off, polished them with the hem of his shirt, and put them back on again. "Jane—"

"Little *sis!*"

There was no mistaking the exuberant voice of Samantha Finch. Normally Jane would have been just as happy to see her, but her timing at this moment was so spectacularly awful that Jane shot her a glare that, if looks could kill, would have taken down a bear at twenty paces.

Sam, of course, paid no attention. She strode through Jane's store like a brisk wind blowing through a quiet town, a huge grin on her face. When she reached her sister's side, she wrapped her up in a bear hug that reminded Jane that Sam was eight inches taller and thirty pounds heavier—every bit of it toned muscle.

"Look at you!" Sam cried out.

Her voice, as always, sounded too loud in the quiet bookstore. Sam always seemed larger than life, so full of exuberant vitality that just being around her could leave Jane feeling sort of wan and pale and tired, a thin sapling next to a mighty oak tree.

"Caleb says you guys have something fab planned for my birthday. This is the big three-oh, Janey. I'm not even sure I want to celebrate it."

"That's good, because what Caleb has in mind will never, ever happen."

Sam gave a mock pout. "Now you've made me *want* whatever it is."

"That's because mentally you're still eight years old."

"I'm rubber and you're glue. Whatever you say bounces off me and—"

"Okay, six years old."

Sam's big personality was enough to distract a person from anything— even a cute customer you had a crush on. But now that the first greeting was over Jane remembered Dan, and when she stole a glance at him, she saw that he was staring at Sam as you might stare at a car wreck on the side of the road, wondering how it happened and unable to take your eyes off it.

Sam must have caught her glance, because she turned the full wattage of her toothy grin on him.

"I'm so sorry, Jane, I interrupted you with a customer." She stuck out a hand, and Dan took it, looking a little dazed. "I'm Samantha," she went on. "Are you a regular?"

"This is just my second time here," he answered. "It's a fantastic shop." He looked from Samantha to Jane. "You two are sisters?"

He sounded dazed, too.

Sam grinned at him. "I know, we don't look anything alike. Except for our eyes," she added. "They're the exact same shade of blue. Cobalt, according to our mother. I've never seen any cobalt, so I just take her word for it."

She turned back to Jane. "I got downtown sooner than I expected, so I stopped by to give you a hug. Also, I wanted to ask if we can have dinner a little earlier than we planned. Like, say, right after you close up shop. I'm starving. Caleb's on his way. He'll meet us there."

"But it's only—" She glanced at the clock on the wall and saw that, somehow, it was five minutes to six. How had that happened?

"You still close at six, right?"

"Yes."

"Okay, then." Sam gave her another huge hug, this one hard enough to make her ribs creak. "I'll see you in fifteen minutes or whenever you get there. Burgers and my kid sister—what could be better?"

And then she blew out of the store like the tail end of a hurricane, the impression so strong that Jane half expected books to blow open, their pages fluttering, as though a literal wind had swept through.

Damn. Jane had been thinking that if Dan asked her out for tonight, she'd have plenty of time to text Sam and Caleb that she needed to reschedule their dinner plans. Now, obviously, that was out of the question.

But that was okay. She and Dan could still do something after dinner, like drinks or coffee. Or they could just make plans for a different day. This wasn't a big deal, just a short-term disappointment.

She turned back to Dan, hoping they could pick up where they'd left off.

He was still staring after her sister, even though she'd left the store and was out of sight. Not that Jane was surprised. It usually took her a few minutes to recover equilibrium after a Sam encounter, and this was Dan's first one.

He turned back to her after a moment.

"Samantha," he said, sounding bemused.

"Yep, that's her name," Jane said.

This might actually be a good thing. They could talk about siblings, since they both obviously had them. And Jane's plans with Sam might lead to a discussion of plans in general, which might lead to a discussion of plans, specifically. As in plans for a date.

"She . . ." Dan trailed off.

Jane nodded. "I know. Sam can be kind of overwhelming."

Dan was quiet for a moment, his eyes almost blank behind his glasses. What was he thinking about? The fact they had only another five minutes? Was he wondering whether to ask her out, or if they should just exchange phone numbers? Or—

The blank look transformed into something else. He put a hand on her shoulder, and she thrilled at the contact. It was the first time they'd touched since yesterday, when their hands had brushed on the counter.

"I was wondering," he said.

Jane's heart began to pound.

"Your sister. Is she seeing anyone?"

Chapter Five

She didn't have a chance to process the question before Kiki came bustling over, chattering about the customer who'd bought every single Nero Wolfe mystery they had, which was like twenty, and now there was a big gap in the mystery section under *S* where Rex Stout had been, and did Jane want her and Felicia to close up tonight?

Jane grasped onto the question mark at the end of that last sentence. There was something in Kiki's chatter that required a response.

"What?"

"I said, do you want us to close up tonight? I heard Sam—I wasn't eavesdropping, but you don't really have to with her, right? She's so *loud*—say that you guys have dinner plans. So if you want me to close up I can. All the customers are gone except—" She looked at Dan. "Not that I'm rushing you out, or anything. I—"

"No, not at all," Dan said. He turned to Jane again. "I could walk you to wherever you're meeting your sister for dinner. If that's all right?"

Everything was happening so fast. What was she supposed to say?

Dan had asked if Samantha was single. He was interested in her. He wanted to walk Jane to the restaurant in the hope of seeing her sister again.

She had no idea how to respond.

"I—"

No. She would say no.

But what reason could she give for saying he couldn't walk her to the burger joint around the corner?

"I was going to do an errand on the way. You don't have to—"

"I don't mind," he said quickly. "Really."

And then, in that moment, Jane felt herself give up.

It wasn't a new sensation. She'd been giving up when it came to Sam for twenty-seven years. Sam had always been too much for her, and she always would be.

"Okay," she said hopelessly, but Dan didn't notice the hopeless-ness—only the acquiescence.

"Wonderful," he said jubilantly. "Are you ready? Should we go?"

She couldn't think of a single excuse to delay. "Sure." Well, there was her purse and her cardigan in the back room. That would give her a moment of privacy to get herself together. "Let me just grab my—"

"Your sweater and purse?" Kiki said, producing them like a genie. "Here you go. I brought them with me so you could head straight out."

Great.

She mustered up a smile for her employee and friend, who was only trying to be nice. "Thanks so much, Kiki. That's great. You've got the keys?"

"Yup."

"I'll see you tomorrow, then."

And less than a minute later, she was walking down the sidewalk with Handsome Dan, just as she'd imagined—except that they were talking about Sam.

"She's so beautiful. I think she's the most beautiful woman I've ever seen."

He wasn't the first guy to think that. He wasn't even the first guy Jane had been interested in who thought that.

"Uh-huh."

"And she's so . . . so *vital*."

"Yep."

"She practically glows. Like she's surrounded by an aura or something. A nimbus of light."

A nimbus of light? Okay, sure.

Dan stopped short, looking down at her in sudden consternation. Around them, bustling pedestrians flowed like a river past a rock.

I'm so sorry, he was going to say. *We obviously had some kind of chemistry going, and now I'm blathering on about your sister. This has to be really uncomfortable for you. Please forgive me.*

"She's dating someone, isn't she? A woman that gorgeous can't be single. And you don't want to tell me. I must sound like such an idiot."

He looked so worried as he looked down at her. His forehead was wrinkled and his eyes were anxious, and she really, really wished she *could* think he was an idiot.

Only she couldn't. She'd been ludicrously wrong about the energy between them, but that wasn't Dan's fault. It was obvious now that any chemistry between them was intellectual. Anything else had been in her head, and she couldn't condemn Dan for being fickle when he hadn't been interested in the first place.

And the truth was, she still really liked him. He was still the bookish geek she'd been drawn to yesterday, and now he was showing this adorably romantic side.

Because of her sister.

"Of course I don't think you're an idiot," she forced herself to say. "And Sam broke up with someone a few months ago. As far as I know she's still single."

His face lit up, making him even more charming and making her feel even worse. He started forward again but stopped midstep.

"I'm sorry, you said you had an errand to do. Where do you need to go?"

Right, her fictional errand.

"You know what? It's fine. I can do it tomorrow. That's the restaurant up ahead, the one with the blue awning. Let's go."

They were on the move again. The setting sun was in her eyes, making her blink. It always seemed brighter between buildings.

"I can't believe I'm only here another week," Dan was saying. "But it doesn't matter. I have to take her to coffee or dinner or—well, something. Anything."

Wait a minute.

"You don't live in New York? You're only here another week?"

Was this the first time he'd mentioned that, or had she missed it somehow?

"Unfortunately, yes. I'm here a few times a year on business, though, and to visit my sister."

"Where do you—"

"There she is! No, I'm wrong. That's not her."

They'd arrived at Kobe-yashi Maru, and Dan was looking through the window at the crowd inside.

She should invite him to join them. Shouldn't she?

Join us for dinner, Dan.

No, Jane, I couldn't possibly intrude like that.

Don't be silly, you wouldn't be intruding. We'd love to have you.

Well, if it's really all right . . .

Then she could spend the next few hours watching the guy she had a crush on make a move on Samantha.

She couldn't do it. It would be the nice thing to do, but she couldn't do it.

"I'd invite you to join us, but I think Sam was counting on a sister thing. You know?"

"Of course," Dan said instantly. He grinned a boyish grin. "And anyway, a part of you must think I'm nuts. I wouldn't encourage me, either."

"That's not it, I promise."

If she really meant that, though, she'd try to help him out.

She took a deep breath. "I'll make lunch plans with Sam for tomorrow." She pointed at the deli across the street. "We'll be there at one o'clock if you want to, you know, casually drop by."

He looked delighted. "Really? I'll be there." He grabbed her hand and shook it. "Thank you, Jane. Have a wonderful evening. I'll see you tomorrow."

"See you tomorrow," she echoed, feeling a little tingle where their palms had met and watching him walk away until he disappeared into the crowd. Then she turned resolutely away and went into the crowded restaurant.

She could see why Caleb disliked this place. He hated crowds, for one thing, and this place was always a crush of people. After the refreshing October air outside it was like a furnace in here, and with the dim lighting and noisy chatter all around her it felt as though she were swimming in a chaotic sea.

Her temples started to throb.

"Those effing Mets . . ."

"Damn mayor . . ."

"And it's not even me being an asshole. I mean, of course there's going to be drama in a divorce, right? But she's a pig. Seriously, you wouldn't believe what she . . ."

"Where should we go after this? There's no movie I feel like seeing, and I'm just so bored by everything, you know?"

Welcome to humanity, she thought as she tried to edge past a knot of millennials in business attire without shoving anyone or being shoved. *We're bored, pissed off, or assholes. Maybe all three at once.*

She thought longingly of her store, always a refuge. The voices there came from the pages of books—thoughtful, funny, sensitive, brilliant, so much more kind and beautiful and articulate than actual people ever seemed to be.

Give her books over real people anytime.

"Little sis! Over here!"

She craned her neck and caught sight of Sam, waving furiously from a corner booth, and Caleb, across the table from her, leaning back with his cowboy hat tipped down so she couldn't see his expression.

Sam really was gorgeous. Perfect skin, long blonde hair, and that toned, athletic body. Even in New York City, where there was no shortage of attractive people, Sam always drew attention.

It was slow work inching through the bar area, where the young and hip were waiting for their cocktails and microbrews. She felt more invisible than usual, noting that none of the guys gave her a second glance as she moved past them. The only time she ever got male attention was when she was with Sam, and then it was only from the wingmen of the guys hoping to meet her sister.

A gap opened in the crowd and she hurried through it, finally able to make a direct line toward her goal. She slid into the booth next to Caleb, elbowing him in the ribs so he'd move over, and tried not to feel like a jealous kid as she smiled at Samantha.

But the hand that squeezed at her heart was all too familiar.

So was the voice that spoke in her head—a little girl's voice, bitter and resentful.

I wish I were an only child.

How could she think such a thing? She wasn't a kid anymore. She was a grown woman with a life of her own—a life she loved, even though Caleb might think it was boring. And she loved her sister.

"I love you," she said under her breath, willing the words to wash away the acid running through her veins. Envy was corrosive, as she knew all too well, and she wouldn't give in to it.

She was a grown woman.

She loved her sister.

"What?"

She focused on Caleb. "What?"

"That's what I said."

"What did you say?"

"I said, 'What?'"

"What?"

"Oh my God," Sam broke in, looking amused and annoyed at the same time. "Janey, you said something, but we didn't hear it. Caleb asked what you'd said. Then we got Abbott and Costello." She paused. "So what did you say?"

"Nothing important," Jane said, grabbing one of the big plastic menus and fixing her eyes on it. There was no way she was going to shout *I love you* at her sister in a crowded hipster burger joint.

"This is why I hate it here," Caleb said, his eyes still hidden under the brim of his hat. "It's not too late to go somewhere else, you know. Or we could order takeout and eat at home."

She actually agreed with him. And that was so annoying she grabbed the hat from his head and put it on her lap. "You shouldn't wear this thing at dinner."

Caleb made a swipe for it, but Jane tossed it to Sam, who put it on the seat next to her.

"Little sis is right. Just pretend you're civilized for an hour, C.B. It won't kill you."

With the hat gone, Jane could see Caleb's expression clearly, and he looked as irritated as she felt. He sat up a little straighter and turned his hazel eyes on her.

"So. How'd it go with Horn-Rims today?"

She might have known he'd ask. God forbid she could just pretend the last hour hadn't happened.

And of course, Sam perked right up. "Horn-Rims? Who's Horn-Rims?"

Jane looked back down at the menu. "A guy."

She could feel Sam's interest and excitement from across the table. Her sister was always telling her to "put herself out there" more.

"A guy you like?"

"Uh-huh."

"That's awesome! Does he know you're interested? Does he like you?"

Jane looked up finally, meeting her sister's happy gaze. What would it be like to be that uncomplicated? For sisterly love and affection to be unmarred by jealousy or insecurity?

She took a deep breath, and then she said words she'd said before. Often, in fact. At fourteen, and seventeen, and twenty, and twenty-three.

"No, he doesn't like me. He likes you."

Chapter Six

Of all the things Caleb had expected Jane to say, that hadn't even been on the list. When the hell had that asshole even seen Sam?

Sam looked confused. "I don't understand. Who—"

Jane shrugged, which was what she did when she was feeling more than she was saying. "He was the customer I was with when you stopped by. You shook his hand."

Sam's forehead scrunched up a little as she thought back. "I remember him. Sure. He *was* wearing horn-rims, wasn't he? But we hardly talked at all. How could he possibly—"

"I guess it was love at first sight."

Jane's voice was flat, but Caleb could hear the bitterness behind it. She sounded sad, too. Forlorn.

A sudden wave of anger swept through him. If Horn-Rims were here right now, he'd punch him in the face.

"It wasn't love at first sight," he said gruffly. "It was lust."

Jane jerked her head around to look at him.

"Of course it was lust," she snapped. "That's the point."

At least when she was pissed she didn't look sad.

"What's the point?"

"Men don't lust after me."

His jaw tightened.

Yes, they do.

For one sickening moment he thought he'd said the words out loud. But Jane had turned back to Sam, who was looking confused and guilty at the same time.

"I told him I'd help him out," Jane was saying. "I said you and I would have lunch at the deli tomorrow, and that he could stop by."

"No way! I mean, of course I'd love to have lunch with you, but I don't want to spend time with this guy. Even if he was my type, which he isn't, you know I'd never go after someone you were interested in."

"I know."

"Little sis, I'm so sorry. I didn't do anything. Honestly, I barely noticed him."

Jane smiled a little. "I know. Believe me, I know."

She shrugged again, and this time the movement meant she was ready to change the subject.

"You know what? It doesn't matter. Let's eat. I'm starved."

Sam looked doubtful, but the waiter came over in time to provide a distraction.

For once Caleb didn't mind the detailed discussion of the day's specials, which included all the ways the restaurant had found to ruin a perfectly good hamburger and the ways they'd found to ruin perfectly good alcohol. It gave him time to study Jane to see if she really was okay.

She seemed to be. She was listening to the waiter as if descriptions of weird condiments were the most fascinating thing she'd ever heard and choosing between them was the only thing on her mind right now.

Sam was definitely okay. Her emotions were big and transparent, and her relief now was as obvious as her worry a minute ago had been. She'd taken Jane at her word and was happy to move on.

Jane was harder to read. She always had been.

Once the waiter left with their orders Sam started to ask about Horn-Rims, but Jane deflected her.

"Tell me about your trip. The pictures you sent were gorgeous, but it's better when you guys describe it."

"You know what would be even more fun? If you actually came with us sometime," Caleb pointed out. "In fact—"

Jane, who knew where he was going with that, smacked him on the arm so hard it actually hurt.

"Not going to happen," she said, glaring at him.

"But—"

"*No.*"

She kept up the glare, and he grinned back at her. When they were arguing, she didn't look sad or wistful.

"She'll never come on one of our expeditions," Sam said. "But at least we can tell her about them." She leaned forward. "Okay, so, the craziest night was near the end of the trip. There was a big thunderstorm, and I mean *big*. It felt like the lightning was right overhead, and some of the people in the group were scared to death. The rain was coming down so hard—"

The waiter brought their drinks while Sam was talking, and Caleb took a long swig of his beer. He listened to Sam and watched Jane, looking for signs that she really was all right. It was so damn hard to tell with her. She was listening to her sister with her chin propped on her hand, taking an occasional sip of her iced tea. In the light of the lamp above their table, her brown braid shone like satin, the loose curls around her ear casting a faint shadow on her cheek.

He remembered the selfie she'd sent last night and the way her hair had looked tumbled around her shoulders. She'd been wearing those Harry Potter pj's, dark blue, and now he wondered what the rich soft brown of her hair would look like against bare skin. If she unbuttoned her pajama top slowly and—

"Did you really do that?"

Both sisters were looking at him, but it was Jane who'd asked the question. For one awful moment he wondered if they knew what he'd been thinking.

Of course that was nuts. Still, his heart was pounding like he'd been caught doing something criminal.

He took a gulp of beer and wiped his mouth with the back of his hand.

"Do what?"

Jane frowned at him. "Have you even been listening? Sam said a twelve-year-old boy broke his leg and you carried him three miles to a place where a medevac helicopter could pick him up."

"Oh. That."

"Yes, that."

She was still frowning at him, and he frowned back. "Why do you look like you're mad at me?"

"It's just . . . that was very heroic of you."

"Which pisses you off for some reason?"

"Of course not. But you could have mentioned it, you know. Now I feel bad for smacking you before and giving you a hard time last night and—"

"I gave you a hard time, too. And what was I supposed to say? Don't yank my chain, I helped a kid with a broken leg?"

Jane's mouth tipped up, and he felt ridiculously glad to see her smile.

"Seriously, though," she said. "I hate thinking about you and Sam in thunderstorms and other dangerous situations. I'm afraid you'll—"

Sam started to laugh, and Jane glared at her. "What's so funny?"

"It's not funny that you care about us," Sam said quickly. "I was just remembering when that movie came out—*127 Hours*?—and you started worrying that one of us was going to get an arm or leg trapped by a boulder and we'd have to self-amputate to save ourselves."

Jane sighed. "I actually hadn't thought about that for a while, but now the images are back in my head. Thanks a lot."

"Anytime, little sis."

The waiter brought their food—bacon cheeseburger for him, burgers with arugula and truffle oil and avocado and seared foie gras and God knew what other weird crap for them—and for a few minutes conversation took a back seat to eating.

The rest of the meal was okay. His burger was actually good—and he'd grown up with cattle ranchers in Colorado, so he knew beef—and the conversation drifted from topic to topic without touching on anything awkward or uncomfortable.

"Heard from Mom lately?" Sam asked while they were waiting for their check.

Jane shook her head. "I think she's still on that meditation retreat. You know she doesn't bring her phone to those."

"And Dad?"

"He called the other night. He's working on some big celebrity case he can't even talk about."

Sam and Jane's parents were definitely an odd couple. Harvey Finch was a high-profile lawyer in Los Angeles, and Nina Finch was a practicing Buddhist and a professor of Japanese studies at UCLA. How they stayed married—and happily so, to all appearances—was a mystery to him.

"Are they coming out for my birthday?"

"Dad can't, but he said he'll make it up to you at Christmas. Mom will be here, though."

Sam grinned. "Dad can't come, huh? That means serious parental guilt for me to leverage. I think it's time to ask for new skis for Christmas. I'll call him tonight and start laying the groundwork." She looked at Caleb. "Is there any chance you'll actually spend Christmas with us for once? You know Mom and Dad would love to have you."

He shook his head. "Nope."

Jane elbowed him in the ribs. "Any chance you'll finally tell us where you *do* spend Christmas?"

"Nope."

The Finches were the kind of family who had holiday traditions. Even if they didn't follow them every year, there was a structure there—built not just out of habit but on mutual trust and affection. He was glad Sam and Jane could take that for granted, glad they looked forward to Christmas every year.

He didn't, but he didn't waste time crying about it—or talking about it.

That didn't stop Sam and Jane from trying, of course. It had become a new part of the Finch holiday tradition. Every year they tried to get Caleb to join them for Christmas dinner or a New Year's Eve party, and every year he declined with thanks.

Nobody, not even his brother, knew where he spent the week between Christmas and New Year's. Caleb had no intention of ever sharing that information with anyone or changing his own holiday tradition.

But even though he made a show of being annoyed when Sam and Jane asked, the truth was, he was touched every single time they did. The fact that the Finches were so willing to include him in the intimacy of their family Christmas meant more to him than he would ever admit, and the fact that he would never take them up on their offer didn't change that.

The waiter arrived with their check. "It's on me," he said, handing over his card.

"No!" Jane said, fishing in her purse—but the waiter was already gone.

He grinned at her, and she glowered back.

"Why can't I ever treat?"

"Because you're too slow."

"That's not true. The last time the three of us got together, I had my card out and ready and you wouldn't let the waiter take it."

"I guess I just want it a little more than you do, pipsqueak." He reached over the table and grabbed his hat from the seat next to Sam. "It's a man's job to pay for the burgers," he intoned in his best cowboy voice, tipping his hat to Jane.

She rolled her eyes. "I don't know how you stand him," she said to Sam.

"He's useful in a crisis. Like if you're leading a hiking expedition and a twelve-year-old boy breaks his leg."

"That's not the only thing I'm good for," Caleb commented. "I can also rub two sticks together to make a fire."

"You should try it with your two IQ points sometime," Jane said.

"Good one," Sam said approvingly, as Caleb signed the check and stuck his card back in his wallet.

"If you ladies are done impugning my intelligence and character, we can get out of here."

Once they were out on the sidewalk, Sam flagged down a taxi.

He felt disappointed. "We're calling it a night? I thought we could get dessert somewhere, or maybe see a movie."

"Not me," Sam said. "I'm meeting Hannah and Michelle for drinks uptown. I told you at dinner, remember?"

"I guess I missed that." He glanced at Jane. "Are you going with them?"

She shook her head. "Things get pretty rowdy when Sam hangs with her college roommates. I'm just going to head home."

Sam climbed into the cab and waved at them through the window. "Talk to you soon, guys!"

Jane stood looking after the taxi until it rounded a corner.

"Love at first sight," she muttered.

Caleb felt a stab of pity, but he was careful not to show it.

He bumped her shoulder with his. "Thought you said it didn't matter."

Pedestrian traffic was flowing past them, and now Jane slid her hands into the pockets of her cardigan and stepped into the stream.

"I lied."

Caleb walked beside her, resisting the urge to put his arm around her shoulders. "Well, you did a pretty good job of hiding it. Kudos."

She shrugged. "If I let Sam see how much it bothered me, she'd offer to do something stupid, like bully Dan into asking me out. That's what she did when I was seventeen and my prom date fell in love with her."

Every time he heard that story, he winced.

"She means well," he said.

"I know. But that only makes it worse."

"How come?"

"Because I can't hate her. Or I shouldn't, anyway. It's not her fault she was born beautiful and athletic."

That hint of bitterness was back, along with that sad, wistful, almost resigned tone.

He grabbed Jane by the arm and pulled her away from the bustling crowd, over to a shop sheltered by an awning. It was a women's clothing boutique, closed for the night, with a light shining on a blue silk dress in the window.

Jane stared up at him. "What are you doing?"

Good question.

"It pisses me off when you talk about how beautiful Sam is."

"Why would that piss you off? It's true."

"Yeah, but . . . that's not the point."

"What *is* the point?"

The point is that you're beautiful, too. In a different way. Your own way.

But if he said that, it might come out sounding like an insult instead of a compliment. Or worse: it might sound like he was making a move on her.

And that was so far out-of-bounds it was over the horizon.

He leaned against the window, took off his hat, and dragged a hand through his hair.

Jane folded her arms and started to say something, but then her gaze shifted to the shop window behind him. Whatever she saw made her smile, and he looked over his shoulder.

"What are you looking at?" he asked.

"This dress. I saw it the morning I met Handsome Dan."

He swiveled his head around again. "Handsome Dan? You don't seriously call him that."

"Why not? He *is* handsome."

"That's the name of a dog."

She blinked. "What are you talking about?"

"The Yale mascot. Handsome Dan. The bulldog?"

Her eyes widened. "Oh my God, you're right. That's why it sounded familiar." She frowned at him. "But how do you know that? You didn't go to Yale."

He and Sam had gone to the University of Colorado, which was where they'd met. "No, but you did."

"The only time you visited was for my graduation. How do you remember the name of their mascot? I didn't even remember that."

He felt defensive. "I happened to remember that detail because it's a sports thing. You forgot it for the same reason."

"I guess." She sighed. "A bulldog. Wow. Okay, I have to stop calling him Handsome Dan."

"Are you kidding? You should call him that all the time."

Jane was looking at the dress again. "The man of my dreams," she murmured.

He frowned. "What?"

She pointed, and he followed the line of her gaze to the sign that hung above the mannequin.

WEAR THIS AND YOU'LL FIND HIM:
THE MAN OF YOUR DREAMS.

"Talk about a hard sell," he muttered, and she laughed.

"That's what I thought, too. But it *is* a beautiful dress."

It seemed pretty ordinary to him—just another Manhattan status symbol, too fancy for real life. There was only one thing about it that seemed exceptional.

"It's the color of your eyes."

He could feel Jane staring at him, and he turned back to face her.

"What?" he asked.

"Nothing. I just . . . didn't know you knew the color of my eyes."

He felt defensive again. "You obviously don't think I notice much." He nodded toward the dress. "Sam's eyes are that color, too."

Jane looked down. "Right," she said after a moment. "Cobalt blue."

"I guess." He paused. "What would you say to walking home?"

She looked confused. "You're walking to Washington Heights? From here?"

"No, I meant you."

"You want me to walk to Brooklyn Heights? From here?"

He grinned. "Not by yourself, pipsqueak. I'll go with you."

"It's at least two miles. Maybe three. I mean, the Brooklyn Bridge is a mile long."

"So?"

"It'll take an hour. Maybe more."

"So?" he said again. "You were complaining about not being athletic a minute ago. Walking is good for you."

"I wasn't complaining about not being athletic. I have no desire to be athletic."

"Walking is still good for you." He took her right hand and placed it in the crook of his left arm, leading her back to the sidewalk like an old-fashioned gentleman escorting a lady. "Let's go."

He expected her to drop his arm immediately, but she didn't. They walked along in silence for a few minutes, but it wasn't an awkward silence.

They kept pace with each other pretty well, considering their height difference. He could feel the warmth of Jane's hand through his shirt, kind of soft and electric at the same time, and the sensation made his heart beat a little quicker.

When they came to the entrance of Jane's usual subway station, they paused by mutual accord. Jane did drop his arm then, and he hoped she couldn't tell how much he missed the contact.

"What's it going to be?" he asked. "Walk or ride?"

She looked down the stairs that led into the subway and then back at him.

Her face was well lit by the ambient glow of the city all around them. But even so, it was hard to tell what she was thinking behind those blue eyes.

That's how it always was with Jane. He'd met her for the first time when he and Sam were seniors at CU, and he'd wondered then what he was wondering now.

What are you thinking?

It wasn't something he usually wondered about people. With most people, you could tell what they were thinking. And if you couldn't, once you talked to them, you found out they hadn't been thinking anything much. The natural world—oceans and mountains and the stars and planets above them—was a million times more interesting than what most of humanity thought about at any given moment.

They were thinking about what they'd had for breakfast and what they might have for dinner. They were thinking about money. They were thinking about sex. They were thinking about football.

Not that there was anything wrong with that stuff. It was just . . . well, predictable. Nothing new or odd or interesting. But with Jane, it was different.

The first time he'd asked her that question, she'd turned to him with a dreamy expression in those blue eyes.

"I was thinking about how science fiction stories have to deal with the problem of language. In *Doctor Who*, all the aliens seem like they're speaking English because the TARDIS gets into your brain and translates, so they just skip right over that problem. But if you think about it, language is one of the most interesting things about contacting an alien race. I mean, can you imagine what trying to understand an alien language would be like? I just read a story about a linguist trying to communicate with aliens, and it makes you think about the whole concept of language, you know? How the way we think is shaped by it, and how learning another language changes us."

He'd just stared at her when she finished, not sure what to say. After a moment she walked away, her eyes still dreamy as the wheels in her mind turned.

His mind didn't work the way Jane's did. He didn't live in his imagination. He preferred to live in the moment, thinking about the problem right in front of him and the decisions he needed to make for the comfort and safety of the groups he took into the wilderness. That felt real to him.

But his next expedition had been to the Danakil Depression in Ethiopia. With two active volcanoes, a bubbling lava lake, geysers, acid ponds, and several mineral deposits, the place looked more like an alien planet than anywhere he'd been on earth.

And he'd found himself thinking about aliens, and what Jane had said about language, and the dreamy, faraway look in her eyes as she talked.

What are you thinking?

This time, here on a Manhattan sidewalk, he was sure he knew the answer. She was thinking that a walk across the Brooklyn Bridge on this perfect October night was a wonderful idea, and that Caleb was a genius for suggesting it.

Okay, she probably wasn't thinking that last part. But he was positive about the first part.

"I think I'll just take the subway tonight. Maybe another time, though."

It actually took him a moment to process that she'd turned him down.

"Huh?"

"I said, maybe another time. Thanks for dinner, Caleb. Have a good night."

And before he could come to grips with her answer, she'd already started down the steps to the subway.

Chapter Seven

Jane stared at her own face reflected in the window across from her as the subway rattled along the track.

Why had she said no to Caleb? It had felt good walking with him after dinner.

More than good, actually. Comfortable and safe but also . . .

Exciting.

Exciting?

She leaned her head back and closed her eyes. That's why she'd said no. After the whole Dan debacle, the last thing she needed was to feel excited about some guy . . . especially when the guy was Caleb.

When you looked in the dictionary under Nerd-Girl Hopeless Crush Objects, the first thing you saw was a picture of Caleb Bryce.

Naturally, she'd had a crush on him when they first met. She was a freshman at Yale, and Sam and Caleb were seniors at the University of Colorado. She spent their entire graduation ceremony staring at Caleb's face. She'd been a normal red-blooded nineteen-year-old girl, and Caleb was . . . well, Caleb. Strong and confident and masculine and a hundred other sexy things.

Of course she hadn't said a word to her sister. Sam always meant well, but she had all the subtlety of a sledgehammer, and the prom-date incident had taught Jane that it was better to have loved and lost than to tell Samantha Finch you liked a guy. That would only lead to Sam cornering him in your kitchen on prom night and threatening to beat him to death with a shovel if he hurt you.

The only thing worse than having a hopeless crush was having your older sister try to help you with it. Since she knew very well the cure would be worse than the disease, Jane had kept her mouth shut about Caleb.

Getting over her crush turned out to be easier than she'd first thought. She and Caleb had nothing in common, and he had this way of looking at her like she had three heads when she talked about things she was interested in. But he was also a really good person—steady and dependable in spite of the wanderlust and need for adventure that seemed to drive him—and as he and Sam turned a little start-up into a thriving business, Caleb had become a part of the family.

The little voice inside her head that commented on Caleb's arms and his butt and his sexy-as-hell grin had faded into the background where it belonged. And the last thing, the *very* last thing, she needed right now was to revive it.

She'd already been humiliated today by an attraction to a guy who didn't feel the same about her. And Dan was a part of her tribe—a bookworm and a Tolkien geek. He even loved *Anne of Green Gables*, for goodness' sake. If she couldn't get a guy like that interested in her, why would she try to level up to the sexy cowboy every woman wanted?

So when those little darts of excitement and pleasure had shot through her body from the place where her hand touched his arm, and when she'd felt tempted to keep going like that all the way to Brooklyn, she'd forced herself to relive the pain of that afternoon.

She practically glows. Like she's surrounded by an aura or something.

Now, as the train pulled away from the last stop before hers, she took a deep breath and squared her shoulders. One more subway stop and the walk home to feel sorry for herself, and then she'd get back to what Anne Shirley had taught her so long ago.

She had an imagination, and she could use it.

She'd sit down at her computer and actually finish the first chapter of the thriller she'd been mapping out in her head. She belonged to a writing group that met once a month, and she'd been putting off giving them anything to critique. The next meeting was in two weeks, and this time she'd have something.

When she got home and settled down at her desk, her eyes fell on one of the quotes she'd posted on the corkboard above her computer.

You must stay drunk on writing so reality cannot destroy you.

That was Ray Bradbury, someone else who understood the power of imagination.

She opened up the folder marked "Mack Connor, PI," flexed her hands over the keyboard like a pianist ready to play, and got to work.

The next two hours passed by in a flash. When she finished chapter one and read it over, it wasn't horrible.

So, she thought in satisfaction as she stood up and stretched her cramped muscles, it had turned out to be a good day after all.

Then her phone buzzed.

She glanced at the screen, saw Caleb's name, and hit Accept.

"What."

"Wow. So that really is how you answer the phone now, huh? Or are you in bed?"

"I'm not in bed yet," she said, walking across the living room to curl up on her couch. "I just find you annoying."

"I wanted to make sure you got home safe." He paused. "And to see how you're doing."

"How I'm doing?"

"After the whole Dan thing."

Two hours ago "the whole Dan thing" had still felt raw. But now, with a good writing session under her belt and the knowledge that

Caleb was miles away in his Washington Heights apartment, she felt better.

She was touched that he had called to ask. To be honest, it showed a lot more sensitivity than she'd thought he was capable of.

Not that Caleb wasn't kind. He was incredibly kind. Kind, generous, dependable, all of that. But sensitive was something different. It required imagination, for one thing, which wasn't exactly Caleb's strong suit.

"I'm fine. I had a good writing night," she added, even though she didn't usually talk to Caleb about her writing. Instead of seeing it as a process that was worth something in itself, he was always pushing her to finish things and submit them to agents and publishers, even when she told him over and over she wasn't ready for that.

"What about you?" she asked quickly, before he could go into his usual pitch. "How are you doing?"

"Me? I'm fine. I'm always fine."

That was definitely the Caleb persona—levelheaded, easygoing, laid-back. Nothing ever seemed to get to him.

Then she remembered their conversation at the restaurant. Caleb had his buttons, too . . . he just didn't talk about them.

She'd gotten used to respecting the boundaries Caleb had put up against certain lines of questioning. His childhood, his parents, where he went every year for Christmas. But Caleb had called to check on her emotional state. Didn't that open the door, just a little bit, for her to check on him?

"Can I ask you a question?"

"Sure," he said.

"Why do you always spend Christmas alone?"

He was silent a moment before he answered.

"That's just how I like it."

Not everything about Caleb's family was off-limits. She'd met his brother once, and Caleb spoke often about his aunt Rosemary. But in all the time she had known him, he'd never once mentioned his mother or father. All she knew was that his aunt had raised him and Hunter from the time Caleb was twelve years old.

"Doesn't your aunt get lonely over the holidays?"

"No. My brother usually makes it to the ranch for Christmas, and the hands are like family. And Rosemary is friends with everyone in town. She doesn't suffer from loneliness, believe me. I visit her a couple times a year, more if I can. I just don't visit at Christmas."

Sam had told Jane that the one time she'd asked Caleb about his parents, he'd snapped her head off. It was one of the only times he'd ever done that.

He'd probably snap her head off, too.

"Caleb?"

"Yeah?"

His voice sounded wary.

What happened to your parents? What happened to you when you were twelve?

But after a moment, she knew she wouldn't ask. It was Caleb's choice to guard his privacy, and she didn't have a good enough reason to knock on that door.

Or maybe she was just a coward.

"Nothing," she said.

"Nothing, huh? You're not going to badger me anymore about the holidays?"

She smiled. "No. I'm all done badgering."

"Good to know. Doing anything exciting tonight?"

"Reading in bed. You?"

"Me? I've got a thrilling evening planned. Beer and basketball."

"You're such a guy."

"Usually when women say that to me, they mean it as a compliment."

"Maybe you should call up one of those women."

"I probably should. But for some reason, I prefer you." He paused. "So what are you going to do about Dan tomorrow?"

"Do? What do you mean?"

"You're supposed to get them together at lunch, right? So what are you going to do instead?"

That was a good question.

"I don't know. I guess I'll tell him she had other plans and couldn't meet me."

"But then he'll just keep mooning over her. You should tell him she's seeing someone."

"I already told him she's single."

"So tell him she just met someone you didn't know about yet. Hell, it might even be true. She's out tonight, isn't she? You know guys always fall all over themselves when Sam's around."

She knew, all right.

"Thanks for reminding me," she said, wincing when she heard the edge in her voice. Hadn't she just told Caleb she was fine?

Time to change the subject.

"Why don't you?" she asked.

"Why don't I what?"

"Fall all over yourself around Sam."

It was something she'd always wondered about but had never brought up. She wouldn't have asked now, but any topic was better than her own feelings about her sister.

"Sam's my partner," Caleb said. "She's practically family."

"But she's so your type. I mean, she's perfect for you. She's beautiful, and you guys have so much in common. What if you guys are soul mates? You could get married and run a business together and—"

"I've never been interested in Sam that way. I just don't feel like that about her."

"Because she's your partner and like family? But—"

"No. I mean, yeah, but that's not why I'm not attracted to her."

"You're not *attracted* to her?"

"You sound shocked. What's the big deal about that?"

"*Everyone's* attracted to Sam. *Everyone.*"

Why was it so important for Caleb to admit he'd fallen under Sam's spell, too?

"What about when you first met her?" she pursued. "When you guys were in college. Before she was your business partner. What did you think then?"

"I thought she was beautiful. And I liked hanging out with her."

"And you wanted to sleep with her."

"No."

"You must have. Every guy who meets Sam wants to sleep with her."

"Nope. Not true. I thought she was beautiful, and I still do, but she doesn't . . ."

"What?"

"Do it for me."

She shouldn't be so happy that there was one guy in the world not head over heels for Sam.

Was she really that jealous and petty? Did she really want so much for there to be some guy, somewhere, who wasn't attracted to her sister?

Not that it mattered. Caleb couldn't be telling the truth. He must sense her envy and insecurity, especially after the whole Dan thing, and was just trying to make her feel better.

"I don't believe you."

He made an exasperated sound, something between a snort and a grunt.

"Fine, don't believe me. We should be talking about you, anyway."

"Talking about me?"

"Yeah. And what you're going to do the next time."

"The next time . . ."

"The next time a guy turns your crank."

"What am I supposed to—"

"You're not going to talk about books. You're not going to try to get to know him. Not right away, anyhow. You're going to flirt."

It was her turn to make an exasperated sound, but hers was between a snort and a sniff.

"What exactly are you saying? That I need remedial flirting lessons?"

"That's a good way to put it, yeah."

"I know how to flirt, Caleb."

"No, you don't."

"Yes, I do."

"Let's hear it, then."

"I'm not going to flirt with you."

"Because you don't know how."

"That's not true!"

"Well, then, show me your moves. What are you wearing, Jane?"

She started to snap at him again and then stopped.

What if she took him up on his challenge?

Maybe she *didn't* know how to flirt. Maybe Caleb *could* teach her something.

She took a deep breath and let it out slowly.

"Nothing."

The silence that followed was short, but it was long enough for Jane to feel like she'd just hurled herself off a cliff.

"Now we're getting somewhere," Caleb said. His voice sounded husky, and she wondered if that was his flirting voice.

Her heart beat faster.

"What happens now?" she asked, the question sounding too loud in the empty silence of her apartment. She lowered her voice. "Aren't you supposed to flirt back or something?"

"Sorry. Yeah." He cleared his throat. "So. If I was there with you . . ." He paused.

"What?" she asked after a moment, her voice so low now it was practically a whisper. "If you were here with me what?"

"Where would you want me to touch you?"

A red wave swept through her, a sudden fever of heat and confusion. It left her heart thudding against her ribs, her cheeks burning, her palms and underarms damp.

She squeezed her eyes shut. "This is a stupid idea."

"It's just practice. It doesn't mean anything."

Not to Caleb. She'd seen him flirt before. He did it well, like he did everything else, but she'd never seen it mean anything to him. She'd never seen him floored by a woman, bowled over, changed. She'd never seen him full of longing or hunger or desperation.

"It just feels weird," she said brusquely. "I can't do it. I can't think of you as anything but . . . well, Caleb."

A short silence. "I thought you were supposed to have such a good imagination?"

"I guess not. Because I can't even imagine being attracted to you."

It was a lie, and not a good one. It was so bad, in fact, that she was sure Caleb would see right through it. She was afraid he'd realize that the truth was the exact opposite—that she *was* attracted to him, and had spent years pretending she wasn't.

"Wow," he said after a moment, speaking lightly. "That's brutal."

"Because you're like family," she said.

He couldn't be buying this, could he?

"Yeah, I get it. So I guess you're on your own, then. With the whole flirting thing."

He *had* bought it.

"Don't worry about me. I'll figure it out."

"Or you'll die alone."

"Now *that's* brutal."

It also sounded like the Caleb she knew, teasing her like a brother. She felt herself relaxing, only now realizing she'd been gripping the phone so hard her knuckles had turned white.

She felt tired, too. What time was it, anyway?

Almost midnight.

"It's past my bedtime. Good night, Caleb."

"Good night, Jane."

◆　◆　◆

Caleb lay in bed with his eyes closed, his body on fire. There was no way he could pretend, now—not to himself. Not anymore.

He wanted Jane.

He wanted her more than he'd ever wanted a woman, and he'd had a vigorous sex drive from the time he was sixteen years old.

He wanted her, and he could never have her, and he'd come really close to fucking up his life tonight. His friendship with Jane, his friendship with Sam, his business and his personal life and everything in between. All because he'd been lying in bed thinking of Jane and his body had hardened in a swift, brutal rush, and he hadn't been able to keep from calling her.

His next expedition couldn't come soon enough. He had too much time on his hands here, time to think about things he shouldn't think about.

Time to screw up the best things in his life.

He took a deep breath and let it out slowly, willing his body to cool down.

Of course there was an easier way to get that done. He could think about Jane, fantasize about Jane until he spilled into the sheets like a teenager. As tight as he was wound right now, it wouldn't take long.

And no one would ever know.

But he couldn't do it. He couldn't give in to that urge. Because the more he gave in, the more he let himself think about Jane like that, the easier it would be to screw up like he'd screwed up tonight. He needed to show a little goddamn discipline, and he needed to start right now.

Don't think about Jane. Don't think about Jane. Don't think about—

He threw off his covers in frustration. Then he levered himself up, swung his legs over the side of the bed, and headed for the bathroom with his jaw tight.

He'd never actually taken a cold shower before, but he would tonight.

And if that didn't work, maybe he could knock himself out with a hammer.

Chapter Eight

Caleb spent the morning on the part of his business he hated—at the tax accountant's talking about receipts and deductible expenses and operating costs. The sheer tedium of it drove Jane from his thoughts for a few hours, which was a relief. But as soon as he left the midtown office building, it all came flooding back.

He had to see her. He had to find out if he'd screwed things up between them. He'd know the second he saw her.

He had one more obligation to get through first: a lunch date with two former clients. They'd fallen in love on one of his expeditions, and they insisted on treating him to an overpriced meal once a year.

Today they met at an Italian place on the Upper East Side. The food was good and the conversation was pleasant, but he was glad when the meal was over and he could flag down a cab.

The snarl of midtown traffic made him want to tear his hair out, but eventually they made it through. It was three o'clock when the taxi pulled up in front of Jane's bookshop. He paid the driver, slammed the door, and strode across the sidewalk to the store.

Once inside the warm, quiet space—an oasis of peace after the street noises outside—he looked around for Jane and didn't see her.

Where the hell was she? Finding Jane in her shop on a weekday afternoon was as sure a bet as finding snow in the Alps or pigeons in the park. Was something wrong? Had she gone home?

Jane had created a few hidden nooks here and there for leather chairs and reading lamps. It was in one of those spots that he found her.

She'd taken off her shoes and pulled her feet up on the chair. Her legs were bent, her arms were wrapped around her shins, and her forehead was resting on her knees.

She sat so still that he froze, as though he'd come upon a woodland creature he didn't want to startle.

There was a lamp with a rose-colored shade beside the chair. It cast a soft pool of light over Jane, making her brown hair shine like polished wood.

He wasn't sure how long he would have stood there in silence, wondering if he was the reason she looked so sad and wishing he could go back in time and stop himself from calling her last night. But then her assistant, manning the register, called out to a customer, "You forgot your purse!"

Jane glanced up, startled, and caught Caleb staring at her.

"Hey," she said, blinking.

"Hey."

A beat went by.

"What are you doing here?" she asked.

"I just, uh, wanted to check on you."

"Check on me?"

Check on us, he wanted to say. *Is everything cool?*

But asking that would make her think about last night, and he didn't want that. What he wanted was proof that last night hadn't changed anything between them.

Which meant he needed to come up with something else.

"To see if you'd read those books I bought. And if you're ready to come hiking for Sam's birthday."

She blinked again. "Oh." She took a deep breath and let it out, and he had a feeling she was coming back from someplace far away. "No, I haven't read the books, and no, I have no desire to go hiking. Sorry."

"What were you thinking about just now?" he asked abruptly. It wasn't the kind of thing he usually asked, and the question sounded strange coming from him.

Jane's eyebrows went up. "You want to know what I'm thinking?"

"You look sad," he said, a little defensively. "Is everything okay?"

Sitting like that, with her arms wrapped around her knees, she looked younger than she was.

"Oh, sure. Everything's great."

He shook his head. "Come on, Jane. Tell me what's going on."

She was quiet for a second. Then: "I met Dan for lunch, and I lied to him."

"Lied to him? About what?"

"About Sam."

"But that was the plan, wasn't it? You were going to tell him she's seeing someone."

"Yes, that was the plan. But I didn't stop there."

"Meaning?"

She rested her chin on her knees. "Meaning I went full Cyrano de Bergerac."

He looked at her for a moment. Then he went into one of the other reading nooks, grabbed the chair from it, hoisted it over his head, and carried it back. He set it down right in front of Jane and sat down.

"I don't know what that means," he said.

She frowned at him, and her skin was so smooth, the crease between her brows was like a ripple on a still pond.

"Cyrano de Bergerac is a soldier and a poet with a really big nose. He loves Roxane, who's an intellectual like him but beautiful. She falls in love with Christian, who's handsome and in love with her, but he's afraid to woo Roxane because he has no intellect or wit and can't write love letters. So Cyrano speaks for him, giving him the letters he wants to write Roxane himself and giving Christian the words to win Roxane's heart."

"I've heard of Cyrano, Jane. But what does he have to do with you?"

She sighed. "I met Dan for lunch, and he was so . . ." She took her arms from around her knees and waved them in the air. "So perfect. Funny and charming and smart and . . ." Her hands fluttered down and settled on the arms of her chair. "Totally infatuated with Sam. I told him she was seeing someone, just like I'd planned, and he was okay with it. Disappointed, of course, but he said she might be single again some-day and he wouldn't give up hope. Then he asked me to tell him about her. What she's like, what she's interested in, what her passions are."

She stopped.

"And?" Caleb prompted after a moment.

"And I told him what I'm like. What I'm interested in. What my passions are."

He was starting to understand.

"Oh."

She spoke quickly. "He doesn't live in New York. I'll probably never see him again. I just . . . I just wanted . . ." She trailed off and shrugged. "I don't know what I wanted." Then suddenly she sat up straight. "No, that's not true. I do know what I wanted. I wanted him to fall in love with me."

As suddenly as she'd jerked upright, she slumped down in her chair again. "And he did," she said softly.

A sick tug inside his gut. "He did?"

"Well, not with me. With a hybrid."

"A what?"

"My brain in Sam's body. A hybrid, like Cyrano and Christian. A person who doesn't exist." She paused. "I watched it happen, Caleb. All the while I was telling him about Sam . . . about me . . . all my stupid ideas about the world . . . I could see him falling in love."

She took a deep breath. "I babbled to him. I never babble. But it didn't seem to matter, you know? He's not going to be with me, and he's not going to be with Sam, so what difference did it make what I told him?" She took another breath. "But it did make a difference. Because he's crazy about the woman I made up."

Something strange was happening inside him. Watching her talk about Horn-Rims like this made him tense and angry and—okay, jealous. What the hell had this asshole ever done to deserve a woman like Jane?

But at the same time, he wanted her to be happy.

He slid his hands into his pockets.

"I can't believe I'm saying this, but it seems like there's a pretty obvious solution here. If this guy liked what you told him, if he's in love with the woman you talked about, then all you have to do now is tell him it was you."

She gripped the arms of the chair. "I can't. Don't you see? I can't do that. Because here's the truth about men—and maybe women, too. Faced with a choice between the inside and the outside, we choose the outside every time. Oh, you might say you wouldn't. You might say it's the inside you care about, the beautiful personality, the mind and the heart and the soul. But you don't see a lot of Miss America Beautiful Soul pageants, do you? Or Miss USA Beautiful Mind? No, you do not. You see swimsuit competitions. And it's not your brain you show off in a bikini, Caleb, in case you didn't know."

"Jane—"

As suddenly as she'd burst out with all that, she stopped. She slumped down in her chair and sighed.

"Oh, it's fine. It sucks, but it's fine. I've read a lot of books, you know?"

Nope, he didn't. If by *you know* she meant *I'm sure you understand what I'm driving at, Caleb.*

"What does that have to do with—"

"All the books I read, and I think I know so much and understand so much and that'll keep me safe or something. But it doesn't. I'm still just a younger sister, the plain one in the family, and no matter what they tell you, that's what people notice. I'll never be as pretty as Sam is, and men like Dan will always want her and not me even though I'm the one they'd really like." She slid down a little farther. "I'm still just as small and petty and jealous and pathetic as I was twenty years ago."

He remembered something he'd told Sam once. He'd said that trying to keep up with Jane when she was on a roll made him feel like a big galumphing dog trying to follow some small, darting creature through a maze she knew perfectly because she lived there.

"That's a good description," Sam had said. "I like that. I know it's irritating, but that's just Jane. You have to just tune her out when she gets like that. Chances are she won't even notice. Just nod a lot."

But it didn't irritate him. He liked it. He liked chasing after her, trying to follow her thought process, even though he knew he was missing at least half of what she was trying to convey.

In this case, he was sure of one thing Jane was conveying: she was running herself down.

He responded to one of the words she'd used. "You're not pathetic." He grabbed onto another word. "And you're not plain. You're—"

Beautiful. He was going to say beautiful. But the word stuck in his throat, full of implications he couldn't speak out loud.

It stuck long enough for Jane to take a deep breath, sit up, and put the conversation behind her with a quick shrug.

"Oh, it doesn't matter. It's fine. I mean, it's just life, you know? Stupid and sad and predictable. Just like me, I guess. But—"

The little bell above the shop door tinkled, and Jane looked over Caleb's shoulder to see who was coming in.

The expression on her face made him twist his head around, and there was Horn-Rims standing at the door, peering around the shop until he spotted Jane.

Before he had time to think, Caleb surged to his feet, shoved his chair out of the way, and stood in front of Jane as Horn-Rims approached.

"What are you doing?" Jane hissed in his ear, which meant she was on her feet, too.

Protecting you, he thought—but from what? Horn-Rims wasn't dangerous. He was just an idiot who thought he was in love with Sam, and he was hurting Jane in the process.

And that's what he was protecting her from, of course. Or what he wanted to protect her from.

Being hurt.

"Get out of the way," Jane muttered, smacking him on the arm as she stepped forward.

"There you are," Horn-Rims said, an eager smile on his face as he strode toward her. He was holding something in his right hand, and when he stretched it out toward Jane, Caleb saw that it was a letter in a cream-colored envelope. *Miss Samantha Finch* was written on it in elegant script.

Horn-Rims came to a stop and handed the letter to Jane. "I came to give this to you. For your sister."

Jane took the envelope and looked down at it for a moment before looking back up. "A letter for Sam?"

Horn-Rims nodded. "Yes. A love letter. I know she's started seeing someone, but if it doesn't work out, will you give it to her?"

"I . . ." Jane paused, took a quick breath, and continued. "Of course I will."

He grinned in relief. "Good. Wonderful. Thank you, Jane." He glanced at Caleb for the first time, still smiling broadly, but Caleb didn't even try to muster up a smile in return.

"That must sound crazy, right? Writing a love letter to a woman you just met?"

"Actually, yeah," Caleb said. "It does sound crazy. In fact, if you want my honest opinion—"

Jane elbowed him in the ribs hard enough to make him grunt.

"You don't want his opinion," she told Dan. "Caleb's not exactly a romantic."

"He just hasn't met the right woman yet," Dan said, smiling once more at Jane before turning to go.

When he was at the door, he turned back. "I'm leaving the city in a few days. When you give the letter to Samantha, would you . . . put in a good word for me?"

Jane didn't say anything for a moment. When the silence stretched into more than a few beats, Caleb nudged her arm with his.

"Sorry. A good word. Yes. Absolutely."

"Thank you, Jane."

And then he was gone.

Jane stared down at the letter in her hand, tracing over the script spelling out her sister's name with the tip of a finger.

Caleb reached out and grabbed the envelope.

"Give me that damn thing."

She tried to snatch it back, but he was too fast for her. He stuck it in his back pocket and folded his arms.

"What are you *doing*?" she demanded. "Give that back!"

"You were looking at it like it's the Holy Grail."

"You don't even know what the Holy Grail is."

"God, you're a snob."

"What?"

"Because I wear a cowboy hat, you assume I've never heard of the Holy Grail or Cyrano de Bergeron."

"Bergerac."

"Whatever. I've heard of him. Books aren't the only way you hear of things."

She was glaring at him. "Fine. I'll never assume you haven't heard of something ever again. Just give me the letter."

"It's not for you."

"It's not for you, either."

"I can give it to Sam. I'll go give it to her right now."

"But he gave it to *me* to give to Sam. And anyway, why do you care? Why won't you let me have it?"

That was a damn good question. Why wouldn't he?

He pulled the letter from his pocket and handed it to her. "Fine. Here it is. But try to keep some perspective."

Jane kept her glare going as she took the letter. "Perspective on what?"

"On the moron who wrote this thing."

"You don't even know what it says."

"Sure I do. I love thee, Samantha, even though I don't know one damn thing about you except what your sister told me, which is actually about her, and the fact that you have blonde hair and a great rack and—"

"Hey!"

He looked down at her. She was still shooting daggers at him with her dark blue eyes, all furious indignation.

"I'm just repeating what you said," he told her.

"What?"

"You were the one who said men will choose the outside over the inside every time."

"I didn't say anything about anyone's rack."

"You talked about bikini competitions. I extrapolated." He paused. "Or am I not supposed to use words like *extrapolate*? Since I'm stupid."

Jane looked startled. "I don't think you're stupid. You know I don't think that, Caleb."

"Yeah? You sure make a lot of digs for someone who thinks I'm intelligent."

Her eyebrows went up. "I didn't realize you were so sensitive."

That sounded a little more like the Jane he knew, and he felt himself relax a little. "Well, now you know. And while we're on the subject, I'm also hurt that you don't think I'm a romantic."

Jane folded her arms. "When did I say that? It's true, but when did I say it?"

"You told Horn-Rims my opinion doesn't matter because I'm not a romantic. Exact words."

"Okay, so I said it," she conceded. "Are you saying you *are* romantic?"

"Sure I am."

"When's the last time you sent a woman flowers?"

"Sending flowers isn't romantic. It's an empty gesture." He pointed a finger at the letter in Jane's hand. "Like that thing."

Her fingers tightened around it. "This isn't an empty gesture. It's romantic. A man pouring his heart out to a woman he fell in love with at first sight."

Caleb pulled off his hat and dragged a hand through his hair. "Jesus. That's not romantic; it's insane. And it's bullshit, because you said yourself the woman he fell in love with wasn't even Sam. It was you."

"It was me in Sam's body."

"Great. So all you need is a body switch, and you'll be all set."

Before she could respond, her assistant popped her head into the nook. "Jane? There's a customer up front with a question I can't answer. It's about Dante's *Inferno*."

"No problem," Jane said. "Considering I'm actually living there at the moment, I should be able to provide detailed directions."

She walked briskly away to help her customer, and Caleb put his borrowed chair back where he'd found it. Then he strolled up to the front of the store and waited until Jane had finished special-ordering a British edition of Dante.

"I have a suggestion," he said when she was free.

He rested his forearms on the counter between them. She did the same, mirroring him, and they looked at each other.

"What?" she asked.

"I think you should give me that letter. And then I think you should forget all about it, forget the idiot who wrote it, and go to a bar tonight to practice flirting with real guys."

A wave of color rose up into her face, and he wished he'd left the last part out. He'd come here to make sure that last night hadn't changed anything between them, and using the word *flirting* would only remind her of their conversation.

"Dan is a real guy. He's not a fantasy I dreamed up."

"Sure he is—just like whatever version of Sam he's got in his head. You don't know anything about him."

"I know more about him than I do about some random guys in a random bar."

"Okay, maybe. But at least out in the wild you'd have a chance to meet someone who's actually attracted to you."

Jane looked down at her clasped hands resting on the counter, but not before he saw the hurt in her eyes.

He winced. "Sorry. I mean, since Horn-Rims has the bad taste to not be attracted to you, wouldn't it make sense to mix it up with other men? They can't all be stupid. Some of them will look at you and see—"

What I do when I look at you.

She looked up again, frowning. "See what?"

He cleared his throat. "A woman they're interested in. Come on, Jane. You know you're not a troll. Horn-Rims is a moron, but that's no excuse to feel sorry for yourself. There are plenty of guys out there ready to fall for you."

He turned his right hand over and held it toward her, palm up. "Hand over that letter."

She shook her head. "I'm going to give it to Sam myself. And I'm going to tell her to give him a chance."

He straightened up and stared at her. "Are you serious?"

"Yes," she said firmly. "I mean, who am I to play God? Maybe they'd be good together. I'll tell Sam what I did, and give her the letter, and tell her to meet him before he leaves the city. Just to see if there's something there. She can explain to him that all that stuff I told him was about me, not her, and tell him who she is. It'll be an icebreaker. Not that Sam needs an icebreaker."

"That guy is the opposite of Sam's type. You know that."

Jane nodded. "Of course I do. He's *my* type. But he doesn't want me, so . . ."

She shrugged.

A knot of frustration tightened in his gut, and he pushed himself away from the counter. "Fine. I think you should give me that stupid thing and forget all about the guy who wrote it, since he doesn't live here and you'll never see him again, but whatever."

He started to turn away and paused, looking back at her. "If Sam actually spends time with this guy and they actually hit it off, you know you'd be totally miserable, right?"

She lifted her chin. "If Sam's happy, I'll be happy."

"You'd have to sit across from them at family dinners."

As he said that, a sudden memory of the last Finch family dinner he'd been to surfaced in his mind. It had been a year ago, and Jane had brought a date.

He'd spent the night trying not to glower at the guy and resisting the urge to challenge him to an arm-wrestling match.

"What's wrong?" Jane asked.

Only then did he realize he'd been staring at her for a minute without saying a word.

"Nothing," he said. "I got distracted. There's some stuff I forgot to do. See you later," he said, turning abruptly and leaving the shop.

Shit. He had a thing for Jane, and it wasn't going away.

But what the hell could he do about it? Jane wasn't a one-night stand person, and he wasn't a relationship person.

He'd given it a shot a few times, but it never worked out. Women started out saying they were fine with him trekking around the world, but they all gave him the same ultimatum in the end: cut the travel way down or call it quits.

He always called it quits.

The fact was, he loved his lifestyle more than he could ever love a woman. He craved the freedom and the adventure. Sam said he was addicted to it, and maybe that was true. But if so, it was an addiction he had no desire to overcome.

And he could never put Jane in a position where she came second.

Of course, that assumed a relationship with her was even an option. As arrogant as he could be when it came to women—at least according to Sam—he wasn't arrogant enough to assume Jane would want to be with him. Hadn't she said last night she couldn't even imagine being attracted to him?

He'd love to believe she was just protesting too much. That she was fighting the same chemistry he was, and for the same reason.

Because she knew they'd be crazy to cross that line.

A woman with a cane and a service dog stepped out of a shop in front of him, and he paused to let them cross the sidewalk. While he waited for them to pass, he glanced at the store window and recognized the display.

WEAR THIS AND YOU'LL FIND HIM:
THE MAN OF YOUR DREAMS.

Did women really fall for that bullshit? With ads like that in stores and magazines, not to mention all the romantic books and movies out there, it was no wonder women like Jane had their heads full of fantasies.

But Jane deserved more than a fantasy. She deserved more than him, too—but at least the attraction he felt for her was real. He could make her feel things she'd never dreamed of, no matter how good her imagination was.

If he had her in his bed, he could make her forget her own name.

The woman with the dog was long gone. Yet here he still was, standing in front of a store window, staring at a dress the exact color of Jane's eyes.

And then he realized he'd made a decision.

Jane might not be a one-night stand person, and he definitely wasn't a relationship person. But he was sick of playing *what if.* He had to find out if Jane felt what he did.

And if the answer was yes?

Then they'd figure out how to deal with it.

Chapter Nine

"I didn't really need your help with that order."

It took Jane a moment to realize that Felicia had spoken to her.

"I'm sorry, what?"

Felicia was restocking the bags under the counter and looking guilty.

"That Dante order. I mean, you're definitely the expert, but I probably could have figured it out."

Jane was confused. "That's all right. I'm always happy to help a customer."

Felicia sat back on her heels. "It was because of Caleb."

Now she was more confused.

"What was because of Caleb?"

"He's the reason I asked for your help. I thought if you were busy he might, I don't know, notice me or something. Talk to me." She sighed. "And of course he didn't. I mean, why would he?"

Slowly the wheels clicked into place. Felicia had a crush on Caleb, and neither she nor Caleb had noticed.

"I'm sorry," she said. "I didn't even realize. Why didn't you say something to me?"

"What, so you could fix us up?" Felicia shook her head as she put the last stack of bags in place. "That would be too much like asking my mom to arrange a date for me."

She brushed her hands on the front of her jeans, looking more like her normal, cheerful self. "Don't worry about it. I mean, he's a reach guy for me, you know?"

"A reach guy?"

"Sure. Like when you apply to colleges? You're supposed to have safety schools, match schools, and reach schools. Caleb's a reach for me."

A wave of depression washed over her. Were people really in categories like that? And did you have to date within your category?

Of course you did. Wasn't that what she'd just told Caleb?

But then why did people always want someone out of reach?

She wanted Dan, and Dan wanted Sam. (It sounded like a Dr. Seuss book.) Meanwhile, Sam wanted . . . well, no one at the moment. Felicia wanted Caleb, and Caleb wanted . . .

She shivered all over, as though a draft of icy air had swept across her skin.

Caleb didn't want her. Reach guys didn't want safety girls, and she would definitely be a safety girl to Caleb. Which just went to show that the looks-based caste system didn't really work, because she didn't want Caleb, either.

Liar.

Okay, maybe she did. Sometimes. But she didn't want him the way she wanted Dan. Dan might be her soul mate, and there was no way Caleb was. Which meant if she felt anything for Caleb besides friendship, it was only . . .

Lust.

Pure, raw, animal lust.

She thought about those hazel eyes looking into hers, that stubbled jaw and those broad shoulders and that sexy grin, and she shivered again.

She wasn't a lust person. She was a mind person. A soul person. A relationship person. When it came to love, she wanted the whole package—or at least the hope of it.

Which meant this whole disturbing attraction-to-Caleb thing had to go back down into her subconscious where it belonged.

"You're not mad at me, are you?" Felicia asked, after Jane had been quiet for a while.

She shook her head quickly. "No, not at all. I was thinking about something else."

Felicia grinned. "Handsome Dan? I saw him come in before."

Handsome Dan. Right.

She'd put his letter in a drawer. Now she pulled it out and set it on the counter.

Miss Samantha Finch.

What did it say? How had he expressed his feelings? Had he written about all the things Jane had told him at lunch, or had he written about Sam's golden hair and creamy skin and perfect body?

Had he written about the outside or the inside?

She'd told Caleb she was going to give the letter to Sam, tell her about the Cyrano thing, and ask her to give Dan a chance.

Caleb had said that could make for some awkward family dinners.

She tried to imagine it. What would it be like if Sam and Dan actually fell in love? Got married? Came to Thanksgiving as a couple, then with kids, then with grandkids?

If all that happened, it would be wonderful.

Wouldn't it?

Because if all that happened, it would mean they were soul mates, after all.

If Caleb were here he'd make that noise that meant he was disgusted, because he didn't believe in soul mates. But Jane did, and Caleb wasn't here to argue with her. So should she go through with her plan? Should she call Sam and tell her—

She didn't have a chance, because Sam called her.

"Hey," she said, sounding rushed and excited. "I know we were supposed to have brunch this weekend and go shopping, but I've been invited to this climbing challenge thing and I really want to go. It's happening upstate, so I'll be gone for . . . I don't know, three days? Is that okay? We can do brunch and everything else next weekend, right? Or do you have plans?"

"I have my writing group next Saturday, but I'm free Sunday," she said automatically, but she was thinking, *If Sam leaves town now, she won't have a chance to meet Dan before he leaves.*

"Fantastic! Next Sunday it is. I'm really psyched about this climb. There's a cash prize for first place, which would make a very nice birthday present for me, and there's going to be an ESPN crew there, too."

"That sounds great. But, Sam—"

Remember that man who fell in love with you at first sight? I met him for lunch and told him I was you, or you were me, or something, which definitely screwed things up, but then he gave me this letter to give to you, and I think maybe you should give him a chance in case you guys really are soul mates—

"I gotta go, kid. We're leaving at four in the morning, and I still have to get my gear together. Stay safe, little sis! I love you!"

"I love you, too," she started to say, but Sam had already ended the call.

On to the next adventure—that was Sam.

She's so vital. She practically glows.

That's what Dan had said. That's why he'd fallen in love with her at first sight.

It wasn't just that she was beautiful. It was that she was so alive.

She was so bright and strong she made everything else seem faded and weak.

Including her.

She felt that familiar being-near-Sam feeling: washed out, tired, insignificant.

There were times being around her was wonderful. Like being around a bonfire on a cold night, you could warm yourself at the flame that was Samantha, absorbing the glowing warmth of her vitality.

But her fire burned so bright it was hard to see anything else near her.

Jane shook her head suddenly. Why was she still comparing herself to Sam after all these years? She'd learned a long time ago how useless that was. The only thing it would accomplish was making her feel bad about herself.

And there was no reason for that. Maybe she didn't climb mountains and sail across oceans and jump out of airplanes, but she had a good life. A *really* good life. She lived in the greatest city in the world, and at twenty-seven she owned her own business. She might have inherited it from her grandparents, but it was still hers—and she'd kept it in the black every year she'd been in charge, which was no mean feat.

But as she told Felicia she was leaving early and gave her the keys to close up, she didn't feel pride in her accomplishments or pleasure in the life she'd made for herself. As she walked down the street toward her subway stop, she felt small and pale and tired and weak—a candle flame beside the conflagration that was Samantha Finch.

Hours later, lying in bed but unable to sleep, she was almost relieved when her phone buzzed and she saw Caleb's name on the screen. She might be confused about him and uncomfortable with the things he made her feel, but he was a distraction from her thoughts. She'd rather feel anything but the smallness and pettiness of jealousy, even a physical attraction she couldn't understand or control.

An attraction that buzzed through her veins the moment she heard his low, rusty voice in her ear.

"Hey there. Still awake?"

"This is the third night in a row you've called me at bedtime. Is this going to be a thing now?"

A low chuckle. "Maybe. Objections?"

"Not yet. I'll let you know." She paused, feeling how wide awake she was now—how awareness crackled across her skin like a thousand pinpricks, filling her with a restless energy.

No other man's voice had this effect on her.

"Jane?"

She was so conscious of her body. Liquid warmth pooled in odd corners, and a tickling sensation teased at her lower belly.

"Yes?"

"Will you have dinner with me?"

She froze. Anxiety drove out all the little darts of pleasure, reminding her that no matter how sexy he was, she didn't want her relationship with Caleb to change. They weren't romantically compatible, and their friendship was too important to screw up.

Of course, she might be reading too much into Caleb's request.

"Dinner?" she asked cautiously.

"Yeah. There's something I want to talk to you about."

It could be anything. Sam's birthday, or . . . well, anything.

"Um . . ."

"It can't be tomorrow, because Sam wants me to go to her climbing thing. What about the day after?"

"Um . . ."

"Eight o'clock at Benvalli's in the Village. I've already made a reservation."

He had?

"Well . . . all right."

The physical connection she'd felt over the past few days was no reason to assume he had anything romantic in mind. After all, hadn't she imagined a physical connection with Dan?

True, those moments with Caleb had felt different. More intense, more visceral, more . . . carnal.

But that didn't mean Caleb had felt them, too.

She had a sudden picture of him in her mind, all lean muscle and physical competence in worn jeans and cowboy boots and—

"What are you wearing?" she asked suddenly.

Dead silence.

Oh God. Had she said that out loud?

"Your hat," she said quickly, her heart pounding. "Are you wearing that stupid cowboy hat right now?"

"No," he said after a moment, sounding amused. "You think I wear my hat to bed?"

Naked except for his hat. Now there was an image she didn't need.

"You wear it everywhere else," she said crisply. "Sam says it's part of your cowboy shtick, like calling women *darlin'*."

He chuckled. "It's not shtick. I am a cowboy, or I used to be. And I've had that hat since I was fourteen years old."

"That doesn't mean you have to wear it all the time. The day I see you without it I'll know it's the end of the world."

"The first sign of the apocalypse?"

"Exactly."

Her heart rate was returning to normal. It was easy, now, to assume that whatever Caleb wanted to talk about at dinner, it didn't have anything to do with the rogue lust that ripped through her every so often when she was around him.

Life would stay safe and predictable and comfortable. Sam and Caleb would go adventuring again in a few weeks—Turkey or Mozambique or Nepal—and she would go back to being happy with what she had.

A quiet life. The life of the mind.

"Hey, Jane?"

His voice was low now, and soft, and it did unspeakable things to her nerve endings.

Suddenly afraid of what he might say next, she spoke before he could.

"Okay, so, good night. I'll see you for dinner at Benvalli's."

And then, before anything else could happen, she ended the call.

◆ ◆ ◆

Two days later, Kiki was telling her she should dress up for dinner.

"There's no dress code," Jane said, using a knife to open the shipping box that had brought them twenty copies of the new J. K. Rowling.

"I know they don't enforce it, but it's a fancy place. I've seen women there in ball gowns and men in tuxedos."

"And I've seen people there in jeans, too."

"Well, that's Manhattan for you. But come on, Jane. When's the last time you got really dressed up for something?"

Okay, it had been a while. But this wasn't a date, because it couldn't be, and because when she'd texted Caleb a few hours ago to ask if he was dressing up he hadn't even answered her. Which was a little weird, because he always answered texts unless he was someplace without Wi-Fi. That happened more with him than with most people, but still.

So what *would* he wear? A tuxedo and a cowboy hat?

"What are you smiling about?" Kiki asked.

I'm imagining Caleb in a tuxedo and cowboy hat. But it was a private thought, with history behind it that would take a while to explain, so she just shook her head.

"Nothing."

But it wasn't nothing. It was a smile, a real smile, and Jane would remember it for a long time.

"Oh, he's here!" Kiki exclaimed. "Didn't you say you were meeting at the restaurant? And your reservation isn't for three hours."

Jane looked up. They *had* said they were meeting at Benvalli's, so she was 90 percent sure that whoever Kiki had seen couldn't be Caleb.

But it was Caleb. He was standing in the doorway of the shop, and he wasn't wearing a tuxedo—or his cowboy hat.

He was in jeans and an old blue shirt, one he'd had for years. It was sunny outside and his hair looked lighter than it usually did. Without the shadow of his hat, she could see his eyes clearly as they stared straight into hers.

They looked like the end of the world.

She grabbed the counter with both hands. Something was wrong.

He didn't look away as he crossed the shop. He walked slowly, as though he hated what he was doing more than he'd ever hated anything in his life.

It seemed like a long time before he reached her. Her hands were flat on the counter, the marble like ice under her palms. He put his hands over hers, covering them completely, and even though his skin was warm it didn't seem to touch her.

His breathing was strange—harsh and uneven, like he'd been hurt internally. His eyes held hers, and she wished she could look away.

Her heart was beating too fast. Instinct told her to hide, to escape before he could say anything, but she couldn't seem to move.

"Jane, I'm so sorry."

Her throat was too dry for her to speak. She stared at him, knowing something awful was coming but not yet knowing what it was.

She had to stop him. "Caleb—" she managed to say.

But she couldn't keep the words from coming.

He took a deep breath. "Sam's dead."

Chapter Ten

Two months after that terrible day, Caleb was standing in line at a coffee shop with his phone pressed to his ear. The woman in front of him was trying to reason with a screaming toddler, and he could feel his temper on a thin wire, ready to snap.

"You have to do something," Nina Finch was saying. "We sent her a plane ticket so she could come home for Christmas, but she wasn't on the flight."

"What do you expect me to do about it?"

His voice was gruff, and he hated himself for that. The Finches had lost their oldest child, and their youngest wasn't talking to them.

She wasn't talking to anyone. Him, least of all.

It had been two months since he'd walked into her store and told her the news. For the rest of his life he'd remember the look in her eyes, the way she'd struggled to break free of him, and the crack of her palm hitting his cheek when she'd finally wrenched away.

"Get out of here," she'd said. "Get out!"

He hadn't. He'd put his arms around her and held her close and made her listen, because she'd have to hear it eventually, and it wouldn't be a kindness to put it off.

It had been an equipment failure, he'd told her. One of Sam's rappel anchors had broken and she'd fallen. She'd died instantly. She hadn't suffered.

"You're lying. She's not dead."

"Sweetheart—"

"Don't call me that. Get out of here. Get out of my sight!"

"I'm not leaving you alone."

And he hadn't. Not until Felicia arrived to handle things at the bookstore so Kiki could take Jane home, promising Caleb she'd stay with her until her parents arrived from California.

He'd known before he'd ever walked into her shop what the price would be. The price of being the one to tell her, the one who broke the news that her sister was dead.

For the rest of their lives, he'd be linked to that moment of shock and grief. And she'd hate him for it.

So he hadn't just lost one sister. He'd lost two.

Nina and Harvey had lost more than he had. They'd lost a child. They deserved compassion and kindness and anything in the world he could do for them.

Unfortunately, there was nothing he could do.

He'd already checked out.

He'd felt it happen a few weeks after the funeral, when Jane still wasn't answering his calls and he was still dealing with the paperwork that resulted from one member of a business partnership dying suddenly. He was Sam's executor, too, which had landed him with even more tasks.

"We should be each other's executors," Sam had said when they'd discussed making wills a few years before. Considering the dangers inherent in their work, they'd decided it was irresponsible not to plan for the unexpected.

"Why would we do that? We've both got family."

"Because I know if Jane died the last thing I'd want to deal with is a will and probate and all that crap. And you know Jane—she cries when those ASPCA commercials come on. She couldn't cope with paperwork if I died. But you'd go right into practical Caleb mode and just take care of everything."

The idea of Sam dying had seemed so ludicrous then. They'd been in a café in Buenos Aires when they'd had this conversation, a shaft of sunlight striking sparks off her golden hair.

So he'd said yes. Even though he'd known that nothing is promised, that anyone can die, even the people who seem most alive.

He supposed he should be glad that Jane and her parents weren't dealing with any of this. But the truth was, he'd checked out. He was counting the days until he'd done everything he was supposed to do, and then he'd be gone. And it would be a long time before he came back.

"I can't fix this for you, Nina. I'm leaving in two days."

"Leaving? Where are you going?"

"Australia."

"For an expedition?"

"Several, actually. I'm going to be based there for a few months, leading treks into the outback." He paused. "If you want to talk to Jane, you can't do it through me. For one thing, she's not taking my calls. For another, I won't be back in New York for a while. I've given up my apartment."

"But, Caleb! Do you know anyone in Australia?"

"Yeah. I know plenty of people."

"You know what I mean. Do you know anyone *well*? Do you have family there or real friends?"

No, thank God.

"If you want to talk to Jane, you'll have to come out here yourself," he said, changing the subject.

"But we always spend the holidays here in LA. Every year. I want her to come home, Caleb. I think it's important, for all of us. We still have three days before Christmas. We can buy her another plane ticket. Please, please, can't you talk to her?"

That kid in front of him was screaming louder than ever.

"Nina—"

"Please, Caleb. Please."

He closed his eyes. "Fine," he said.

"What?"

"I said fine!"

"Oh, thank goodness. Call me and tell me how it goes."

And before he could take the offer back, Jane's mother ended the call.

Goddamn it.

Using the phone would be no good—Jane wouldn't answer. He'd stopped by the shop a few times, but she hadn't been there, and Kiki had said her hours had been irregular since the funeral.

If he wanted to see her, he'd have to go to her apartment—the one thing he'd told himself he wouldn't do.

It was one thing to call someone who wouldn't answer or go by their place of work hoping to see them. But to go to their home, knowing they hated the sight of you . . . knowing you'd probably get the door slammed in your face . . .

Oh well, what the hell. What was one more bad memory to file away in the room marked "Don't Look in Here"?

He finally got his coffee, wrapped his cold hands around it, and took it with him on the subway to Brooklyn.

The last time he'd seen Jane was at the funeral. Sam had asked to be cremated, so there was no gravesite horror to go through—just a memorial service for friends and family at a church Sam had liked, even though her work schedule had meant she wasn't a regular attendee.

It had been a perfect October day, so beautiful it had hurt . . . and as different from today as it was possible to be.

Today was funeral weather. Gray and cold and raw, the sidewalks covered with a mix of icy slush and dirty snow. Once he left the subway station, the only warmth anywhere was in the cardboard cup he held between his hands, and even that was dissipating.

After two blocks it was gone completely. He threw it in a trash bin without having taken a single sip.

Another ten minutes and he was at Jane's place.

He was heartened a little by her tree-lined block. This was a neighborhood people cared about, the kind of place people decorated for the holidays. There were wreaths and red ribbons and little twinkling lights everywhere, and in the downstairs windows of Jane's building a child had hung homemade snowflakes and paper chains.

Maybe Jane had absorbed some of the holiday cheer in spite of herself.

He walked up her stoop as someone else was coming out, so he didn't have to get buzzed into the lobby. The Christmas theme continued here with gold and silver bows on all the mailboxes.

One of the mailboxes was stuffed full, as though the owner were away on vacation.

He went close enough to read the name and saw that it was Jane's.

Great. What if she wasn't here? What if she'd gone away someplace?

Her apartment was on the third floor. He went up the stairs slowly, wondering what he'd do if she wasn't home. Wait? He might have to wait a long time. Try to track her down? She'd have to have told Kiki and Felicia where she'd gone.

There were two apartments on each floor. The door across from Jane's had a big wreath hung on it and a red-and-green welcome mat proclaiming "Happy Holidays!" on the floor in front of it.

Jane's door was unadorned. He knocked, but he was almost certain now that Jane wasn't home. He was already trying to think of a plan B when he heard a voice on the other side of the door.

"Who is it?"

The voice sounded strange—a little creaky, like an unused gate. But it was definitely Jane's.

"It's Caleb. Let me in."

Now that he'd heard her voice, he was ready to settle in for a siege if necessary, to get a look at her and make sure she was all right.

But it didn't take a fight. The door swung open, and there was Jane, standing in the doorway and looking at him.

She was drunk. Even if she hadn't been holding a bottle of vodka, he would have known from the vague, bleary look in her eyes.

Her feet were bare, and so were her legs. She was wearing an old white T-shirt, a little too small for her, and when she lifted a hand to brush her hair off her face it rode up enough that he could see her underwear—white cotton with bright red candy cane stripes.

In all the time he'd known her, he'd never seen Jane look like this.

"Jesus," he said.

Jane nodded. "He has a birthday coming up." She pulled up her T-shirt to give him another glimpse of her panties. "See? I'm festive."

She let go of her T-shirt and leaned toward him, resting the hand not holding the vodka in the center of his chest. "Actually," she said confidentially, her face close enough that he could smell the alcohol on her breath, "I'm not wearing these to be festive. My aunt sent them for Christmas, and I put them on because I'm out of clean underwear."

He looked down at her for a moment and then over her shoulder at her apartment. It was a mess, the kitchen filled with dirty dishes and the living room crowded with old pizza boxes and Chinese takeout containers. Through the bedroom door he could see laundry piled up on the floor.

He looked back at Jane. "Invite me in," he said.

She blinked up at him for a moment, her eyes not quite focused. Then she took a step back and gestured grandly with the vodka bottle. "Won't you please come in?"

He closed the door behind him, went to the middle of the living room, and turned to face her again.

"Okay," he said. "Now say, 'Caleb, you have my permission to clean this place up.'"

"Caleb, you have my—" She stopped. "Wait a minute. You totally do *not* have my permission."

"Jane—"

She threw the bottle of vodka onto the sofa and stormed up to within a few inches of him.

"What's wrong with you? Why would you say that? There's nothing wrong with my apartment. How dare you come in here and tell me my sister's dead?"

She heard the words at the same time he did. He watched it happen with a sick feeling in his stomach, and when her eyes widened and she stared at him, all he could do was stare back.

"I didn't mean that," she whispered, and his heart clenched in his chest.

He closed the space between them and put his hands on her shoulders. "Jane—"

She shrugged away from him. "It's not your fault. It's my fault."

She turned her back and took one uncertain step, and then another. He'd never seen a human being look so utterly lost.

He came up beside her and took her hand. Then he tugged on it, gently, and led her over to the sofa. He shoved the pizza boxes off to clear a space, and then he sat down, pulling on her hand until she sat down beside him.

"That's not true," he said. "It's no one's fault."

She looked at him for a moment, her face twisting as her eyes filled with tears she refused to shed.

"I was going to tell her about Dan. I was going to give her the letter and tell her to give him a chance. I could have stopped her from going on that trip." She took a deep breath. "But I didn't tell her, because I was jealous."

"Telling her about Dan wouldn't have stopped her from going. Nothing would have. Nothing ever stopped Sam, Jane. You know that."

"She would have stayed if I'd asked her to. She loved me, and if I'd asked her to stay she would have."

"Jane—"

"Do you know what her last words to me were?" Her lips trembled for a moment, and she took a deep breath. "'Stay safe, little sis. I love you.'"

His heart clenched again. *Sam*, he thought. *Oh, Sam.*

Jane pressed her hands to her temples as though her head had started to throb. "She always told me to stay safe. Why? When have I ever done anything but stay safe? She was the one who needed to hear that. But I never told her."

"She wouldn't have listened. You told her you loved her, Jane. That's what's important."

She shook her head. "But I didn't. I started to say I love you, too, but she was gone. I never got a chance to say the words."

"You told her plenty of times, Jane. She knew. You know she did."

Her hands pressed harder, as though she were trying to crush her own skull between them.

He grabbed her wrists and pulled her hands away. "Stop that."

"If she read my mind, she would have known the truth."

Her hands felt so small, so cold, so fragile. He held them tighter, trying to will some of his own body's warmth into her.

"She did know the truth. You loved her, and she knew it."

Jane shook her head. "But I didn't," she whispered. "Not really. The truth is, I was jealous. She was beautiful and alive, and I was jealous of her, and I wish I was dead."

Up until that point, the only thing Caleb had felt was pity and sorrow. But now, a whiplash of anger cut through the pain.

He let go of Jane's hands, grabbed her shoulders, and shook her.

"Is that why you're living like this? Are you trying to kill yourself?"

The shock of his sudden fury seemed to wake her up a little. Her eyes were a little clearer, a little more focused, as she stared at him.

"What are you talking about? What's wrong with the way I'm living?"

He gestured around the apartment. "Are you kidding? The place is a mess." He gestured toward her. "*You're* a mess. You stink, Jane. When's the last time you took a goddamn shower? Last month?"

The harshness of his words woke her up a little more.

"I don't know."

"Well, you're going to take one now. Come on."

He surged to his feet and pulled her up with him, leading her to the bathroom. She stumbled after him, but he kept her on her feet until they were there, and then he closed the door behind them.

It wasn't as messy in here as in the rest of the apartment. There were even clean towels hanging on the rack, maybe because it really had been a while since Jane had taken a shower.

"I thought I was exaggerating, but how long *has* it been?"

The blinds had been closed in the living room, and the only light had come from a lamp on a side table. In here, the cold gray light of a winter afternoon seemed almost cheery in comparison.

"Since what?"

"Since you were clean."

Jane sat down on the toilet seat. "I told you I don't know."

There was a radiator in here, and with the door closed the small space was warming up.

"This is actually the nicest room in your apartment right now," he said to her. "So you're going to stay in here while I take care of some stuff out there."

He went over to the tub, closed the stopper, and turned on the water, fiddling with the faucets until he got the right temperature—hot, but not too hot.

"A bath will feel even better than a shower."

He turned back to Jane as the tub began to fill. He started to ask if she had any bubble bath, but he forgot the question when he saw the look on her face.

"What's wrong?"

She wrapped her arms around herself as she looked down at the floor. There was a rug, soft and white and fluffy, but she took her feet off it and rested them on the cold tile instead. "You said a bath will feel even better."

"Yeah."

"You don't understand. You don't understand anything."

"What don't I understand?"

She looked up at him again, and the expression on her face tore at his heart.

"I don't want to feel better."

He knelt down on the floor and put his hands on her knees. Their faces were level now, and he looked straight into her eyes.

"You're wrong, sweetheart. I do understand. I know you don't want to feel better. But I'm in charge right now, and you don't have a choice. Do you have any bubble bath?"

She shook her head.

"That's okay. The bath will still feel good. I'm going to wait here until the tub is full, and then I'm going to turn my back while you get in, so I know you did."

He thought for a second she might argue, but then her shoulders slumped and she looked down at the floor again.

For the moment, her depression and exhaustion actually gave him an advantage. They didn't leave her with enough strength to fight him.

He didn't say anything else until the bath was ready. Then he turned off the faucets and went to the door, standing facing it with his back to the room.

"I'm not leaving until you get in," he said.

A moment of silence. Then: "Fine."

Another moment passed, and then he heard the faint splashing that meant she was stepping into the tub.

"Stay in until your fingers get pruny. And if you don't use the soap and shampoo, we'll do this all over again."

"My God, you're bossy."

He started to answer, but a sudden realization made the words stick in his throat.

Jane was naked.

At least, he assumed she was. Considering she was still under the influence of alcohol, he supposed it was possible she hadn't bothered to undress before getting into the tub.

It was the last thing he should be thinking about right now. And as if to confirm that truth, Jane's voice came from behind him.

"You can go now, Caleb. I'm in the damn tub. I'm putting soap on a washcloth. Go away."

"Right." The word came out as a kind of croak, and he opened the door and closed it behind him.

He stood there a moment, breathing deep and trying not to imagine Jane naked and covered in water.

It was a good thing he had a big job waiting for him.

When he saw how bare the fridge and the cupboards were, he decided he should go to the grocery store on the corner before he did anything else. But then it occurred to him that they might make deliveries, which would save time, and when he called them up they confirmed it.

He placed an order for more food than Jane could eat in a week.

He spent the next ten minutes taking care of the easy stuff—bagging up the pizza boxes and other trash. Then he gathered up the laundry from Jane's bedroom and put a load in the little washer behind the door in her kitchen.

There was a clean set of sheets in the bottom drawer of her bureau, so he was able to make her bed. He also found her Harry Potter pajamas neatly folded in another drawer, and he wondered for a moment why she was wearing a smelly old T-shirt.

The answer, of course, was obvious. She loved the pajamas, and wearing them would have felt good.

Something she didn't think she deserved.

She really was out of clean underwear, though—except for the other two pairs in the holiday three-pack sent by her aunt, which was on the coffee table in the living room beside a glitter-covered Christmas card.

He pulled out the pair covered in green holly and red berries and carried them, along with the Harry Potter pajamas, over to the bathroom.

He knocked on the door.

"How's it going in there?"

"I'm pruny."

He smiled for the first time that day.

"Well, good. You ready to get out?"

"I suppose."

"I've got clean clothes for you to put on. I'm going to open the door a crack and drop them on the floor."

"It's very considerate of you to protect my modesty," she said, sounding a little like the old Jane again. "That's definitely something I'm worried about right now."

"Okay, then, I'll just walk right in."

He turned the doorknob and she squealed.

"Caleb!"

He smiled again. "Don't worry," he said, opening the door just wide enough to drop the clothes on the floor before closing it again. "Your modesty is safe with me."

The groceries arrived, and after he put the bags on the counter, he filled Jane's copper kettle and turned the burner on. As he put the food away, it started to sing.

He'd included chamomile tea and honey in his grocery order, and as he made a cup for Jane and one for himself it occurred to him that this had been his mother's way of coping with tragedy and hard times. Considering he'd never before looked to his mother as an example to follow, he must be pretty damn desperate.

It wasn't just his mother he was looking to, though. As he toasted white bread and spread butter on it, he remembered something Sam had told him once when they were on a cold mountaintop together with the temperature dropping. They'd been talking about favorite foods to keep their spirits up.

"Hot buttered toast," Sam had said. "That's what Jane and I decided was the most comforting thing, back when we were kids. Well, that plus puppies and kittens. But if you can't get puppies and kittens, hot buttered toast is pretty good."

And so when Jane emerged from the bathroom in her Harry Potter pajamas with a freshly scrubbed face and wet hair, he had tea and hot buttered toast ready for her.

She looked less happy to see the tray on the coffee table than he'd hoped she would.

"I'm feeling kind of queasy," she said. "I don't think I can eat anything."

"You're queasy because of all the vodka."

"Thanks for that brilliant analysis. Where is my vodka, by the way?"

"Down the drain."

She looked indignant. "Hey! That belonged to me, not you."

"Now it belongs to the alligators in the sewers." He pulled her down on the couch beside him and nudged the tray closer to her. "Have a bite of toast and a sip of tea. It won't kill you."

She looked at the mug he handed her with distaste, but at least she took a sip.

"Can I ask you something?" he said.

She nodded, and he pointed to the one thing on the coffee table—the whole apartment, really—that looked intentional instead of chaotic. Several sheets of brightly colored paper, a few of them folded into shapes that weren't yet recognizable.

"What's this? Origami?"

She looked where he was pointing and then away. "Yes. It's stupid."

"What were you trying to make?"

She shrugged. "Paper cranes. I haven't done one for years, though, and I've forgotten how. Like I said, it's stupid."

"What is?"

She took another sip of tea. "There was this story Sam and I both read when we were kids—one of the few books we both liked. It was about this girl who lived near Hiroshima when the atomic bomb was dropped. There's a legend in Japan that whoever folds a thousand paper cranes will be granted one wish. This girl developed leukemia, and she tried to fold a thousand paper cranes before she died. She didn't make it. I tried a couple times to get to a thousand when I was a kid, but I never finished. The closest I ever got was two hundred."

He looked at the sheets of paper. "I don't think there's enough here to make a thousand."

"Nope. And I don't know what I'd wish for even if I did."

She leaned forward and swept the paper and her half-finished cranes onto the floor, and Caleb resisted the urge to pick them up.

"I think I'm still drunk," she muttered.

"Good thing you don't have a driver's license."

"I feel like shit."

"Eating and drinking will help. Also aspirin."

"I don't have any aspirin."

"I ordered some from the grocery store."

He went over to the kitchen counter, grabbed the bottle, and came back with two white pills.

"Here you go."

Jane swallowed them dry and then gulped down some tea.

"You think of everything," she said.

"Not everything."

"Really? What didn't you think of?"

He looked at her for a moment and then away. He rose to his feet, went over to the window, and opened the blinds.

Night had fallen. In the light of the street lamps he could see snow coming down.

He turned back. "I didn't think to check Sam's climbing equipment before her trip."

Jane froze.

For a moment they just looked at each other. Then Jane said, "That's stupid. You know that's stupid."

"No more stupid than you thinking you killed your sister because you didn't make her stay in New York to meet some guy who thought he was in love with her. Or because you felt jealous of her once in a while."

Jane started to tremble, and he had to resist the urge to go over and put his arms around her.

"Get out," she said, and her voice was shaking, too.

"As soon as you eat something and go to bed, I will."

"You can't blackmail me into . . ."

"Into what? Taking care of yourself? I'm doing it right now. You want me gone? Eat something and go to bed. That's what it'll take." He paused. "I've actually got better things to do than be here, you know. I'm going to Australia in two days."

Her head jerked up like someone had given her an uppercut to the jaw.

"Australia? You're going to Australia?"

He nodded. "So as soon as you eat some goddamn toast, I'll be out of your hair."

She'd stopped trembling, except for the slightest quiver in her lower lip. Almost as though his awareness made her aware of it, too, she pressed her lips together in a firm line, stilling that tiny movement.

"Fine by me," she said.

Then she picked up a piece of toast and started to eat.

Chapter Eleven

When Jane woke up, she was sober.

She hadn't been this sober for a few days. As she lay awake in the dark, turning her head to see the snow falling in the light of the streetlamps outside her window, she knew why she'd been avoiding this feeling.

Reality pressed on her like a heavy stone.

There was a hole in the world where Sam had been. Not just in her life, but in the world. That's how bright and beautiful and alive her sister had been.

The sister who was left was only a shadow. She was dull and gray and weak and tired, and she would have drunk herself into a stupor—or worse—if Caleb hadn't come along.

Caleb.

Having him around, even pissing her off and bossing her around, had been wonderful. And now he was gone, heading for Australia, and she'd probably never see him again.

She squeezed her eyes closed, but it was too late to stop the tears that leaked out, slipping down her cheeks like the drip, drip, drip of melting ice.

Having him here had reminded her she could still feel.

He'd made her take a bath. He'd made her drink tea and eat hot buttered toast.

Now he was gone, and she hadn't thanked him. She hadn't said one nice thing to him.

She rolled over onto her stomach and cried into her pillow. She cried for Sam, for all the things she wished she could tell her. *I'm sorry I was jealous of you. I love you. I miss you.* She cried because Caleb was gone, and for the things she hadn't told him. *Thank you for trying to help me. Be safe. I love you.*

She spent her life surrounded by words. Millions upon millions of words, books spanning centuries. And yet, when it really counted—for the people who really counted—she couldn't manage to say the simplest, truest things.

After a while, she stopped crying. Not because she felt better, but because there couldn't be any more tears left in the universe.

She sat up in bed and rubbed her eyes. They felt sore and swollen, and she wanted to go to the bathroom and splash her face.

But if she got out of bed, she'd feel the emptiness of her apartment without Caleb in it. He'd been like a fire crackling on a hearth, giving out life and heat that could warm anyone—even her.

And now he was gone, and she hadn't thanked him. She was selfish and sad and small and weak, and she hadn't thanked Caleb or wished him a safe journey.

Stay safe, Caleb. I love you.

Loneliness and regret spilled out of her heart and into the empty apartment, echoing in the stillness and silence around her. The only thing that could drive it away was alcohol, and Caleb had dumped hers down the drain.

It was too late for that, anyway. Caleb had pulled her out of that morass, and she knew that however tempted she might feel, she wouldn't slide back into it.

She took a deep breath. What was there left to do now but put one foot in front of the other and go through the necessities of being alive?

She might as well start by going to the bathroom.

Another deep breath, and then she got out of bed. The floor was cold under her feet, and she felt a moment's resentment for the loss of her alcohol haze. With vodka in her veins she hadn't felt the cold.

She crossed the room to her bedroom door, noticing for the first time that it was closed.

Which was weird. When you lived alone, you didn't bother to close your bedroom door.

She turned the knob and pushed the door open, and then she froze.

Caleb was sleeping on her sofa.

For just one second, she wondered if she'd lost her grip on reality. During the first hours after learning about Sam, she'd pushed away the truth so hard she felt like a character in *Somewhere in Time*, wishing herself into the past with enough force to make it happen.

It hadn't happened, of course. She hadn't gone back into the past to undo Sam's death.

She closed her eyes and opened them again.

The silence wasn't only in her apartment. It was outside, too, the snow falling in a still night without wind, soft and quiet and blanketing the world.

The thick flakes made the streetlights seem diffuse. A faint, almost eerie glow came into her apartment through the blinds Caleb had opened yesterday.

She took a step forward, and then another. She hadn't wished Caleb into existence. He was really here, snoring on her sofa with her extra blanket covering him.

After she'd finished her tea and toast he'd put her to bed, assuring her he would leave as promised. Instead, he'd slept on her couch to make sure she was okay.

It took seven more steps to reach him. She sat down on the coffee table, staring down at his face as he slept.

His hair was rumpled against the sofa cushion, and his skin looked paler than usual in the dim light of the snowstorm. His jaw was stubbled, but the lines of it—and the lines of his mouth—were softer in sleep than when he was awake.

She reached out a hand and cupped the side of his face.

It happened so suddenly she didn't even have time to gasp. Caleb surged up to a sitting position and grabbed her wrist so hard it hurt, staring at her with wide eyes.

Everything stopped, including her breath.

Feeling and sensation swept through her. Her whole body felt like a frozen limb coming back to life, the blood tingling and smarting as it returned.

Longing and desire were a sudden fever inside her. She felt so alive it hurt, a glorious agony of being, of wanting.

Of wanting Caleb.

Every lustful thought she'd pushed deep into her subconscious came rushing to the surface, every wave of desire, every tremble, every quiver she'd ever felt when he flashed his lazy grin or tugged on her braid.

Her heart was pounding so hard it shook her body.

She had to get away. But the moment she tried to break his hold, he grabbed her other wrist just as hard.

His hands were like iron. What was happening? Caleb, always so calm and imperturbable, looked like he was in the grip of something he couldn't handle. Something stronger than he was.

She hadn't known anything was stronger than he was.

Seeing the maelstrom in his eyes was more terrifying than feeling it herself.

She tried to pull away again, but she might as well have tried to break handcuffs.

Neither of them spoke. They were surrounded by silence, three-in-the-morning silence and snow-falling-on-snow silence, and the only people in the whole world were her and Caleb.

She'd never realized how much his eyes concealed. She knew it now because whatever he'd hidden behind was gone. She could see everything. Old feelings and new feelings, grief and loneliness and raw, naked hunger.

It wasn't too late to stop this. All she had to do was speak, and order would be restored to the universe. All this emotion would sink back down where it belonged.

I'm sorry I woke you up. I didn't realize you were still here.

That's all she had to do. Say something normal, something rational. Any words could dispel this charged silence, this utter stillness, and the madness that lay coiled within it.

She opened her mouth, but no words came out. Only her breath, ragged and shallow.

A deep breath would stop this. A deep breath would calm her, restore her, pull her back from the brink.

But there was a weight on her chest, squeezing her lungs. Short breaths, shallow breaths, were all she could manage.

Her heart would burst through the vise that held her. It was pounding so hard she could hear it, a wild drumbeat in her veins, a tide of blood rushing in her ears.

Maybe she would pass out. Between her racing heart and her stunted breath, maybe she could just lose consciousness and escape that way.

She'd been trying to escape for so long.

Caleb's grip on her wrists didn't loosen. Under his T-shirt, his chest and arms were as rigid as iron.

She couldn't speak, but maybe he could. His words would have the same power hers did, to shatter this moment and restore them to what should be.

Jesus, darlin'. You scared the crap out of me.

But he didn't say anything.

Instead, slowly, he began to pull her toward him.

Tell me I scared the crap out of you. Tell me to go back to bed. Tell me you'll see me in the morning.

Her thoughts became frantic, as frantic as her heart thudding against her ribs.

Tell me . . . tell me . . .

Tell me this isn't happening. Tell me I'm dreaming. Tell me you're not here and I'm not here and none of this is real.

Tell me you and I are nothing more than friends.

But he didn't speak. He pulled her off the coffee table and onto the couch, and then onto him, her knees finding space on either side of his hips.

Stillness all around them, so profound it seemed like a new element. Earth, air, fire, water, silence.

And Caleb was as distinct and elemental as any of those.

The only light in the room was the eerie glow of snow and streetlamps, but she felt as though she'd never seen Caleb so clearly. His soft brown hair, the skeptical quirk of his brows, his strong nose and harsh cheekbones and stubbled jaw. The faint sheen of perspiration on his upper lip, the glitter of his pupils, the almost imperceptible twitch of his facial muscles as he stared up at her.

His chest rose and fell with every harsh breath. His hands still gripped her wrists. It seemed like they stayed that way forever, frozen in the stillness and surrounded by a city muffled in snow.

Her knees sank into the cushions on either side of his hips, bringing them closer. Heat coiled into her belly from the place where their bodies touched, the hard ridge of him pressing against her until the urge to move, to surge into him, was so strong she was afraid of it.

She couldn't do that. She couldn't. They hadn't done anything yet, and it wasn't too late to stop this.

Tell me nothing is different between us. Tell me we're still the same people we used to be. Tell me . . . tell me . . .

Tell me Sam's still alive.

Oh God.

The echo of Sam's name in her mind filled her with sudden rage. Rage that her sister was dead, rage at herself for being alive, rage that the universe was so screwed up it had taken Sam and left her behind.

And rage at Caleb for coming to her apartment and making her feel so much, after she'd worked so hard to feel nothing.

Caleb was making her want things and hunger for things and—

No. Not things.

Him.

She wanted him.

For the first time in weeks she wanted something she could actually have.

She started to tremble. And then, suddenly, Caleb let go of her wrists.

"You're crying. I'm sorry." He rubbed his eyes with a shaking hand. "God, I'm so sorry."

He'd spoken. Wasn't that what she'd wanted? One of them to speak and break the spell?

She hadn't realized she was crying. Now she brought her fingers to her cheek and felt the wetness there.

There was a crack in her heart. A fault line. And if a single drop of water got into that space, she would break apart.

"I hate you," she whispered.

A flash of pain across his face. They were both in pain, and that was good.

It would be evil to feel anything but pain when Sam was dead. The only other choice was to feel nothing at all.

But Caleb had made that impossible. He'd come here and made her feel.

"I hate you," she said again. Her voice was louder this time. "I hate you."

Every time she spoke the words it was like a whiplash, but she wasn't sure who was struck by it.

"I hate you. I hate you. I—"

Caleb surged upward, grabbing her shoulders and twisting their bodies with a single savage motion.

And then she was on her back, the weight of Caleb pressing her into the sofa and the blanket tangled around both their legs. The word *hate* was still a breath in her lungs when he kissed her.

His mouth was hard, his lips soft.

She wanted him to kiss her harder. She wanted her mouth bruised, her lips cut and split by his teeth. She slid her arms around his neck and pulled herself into him. He urged her lips apart and thrust his tongue against hers, the taste of him salty and feverish and desperate.

A thousand tiny shocks prickled her skin. His stubble scraped her cheeks, and the sensation sent a restless surge through her body.

He jerked away from her. She stared up at him in confusion and then realized with a horrified jolt that she'd slid her hands under his T-shirt and raked his back with her nails.

"Oh God, I'm sorry. I'm so sorry. I'm—"

He grabbed her pajama top and pulled it over her head, cutting off her words. Cool air puckered her bare nipples as Caleb reared back for an instant, tugging off his own shirt, and then they were pressed together skin to skin.

The hard muscles of his chest crushed her breasts flat as he kissed her again.

Hunger was an electric current between them. Their hips thrust together, but there were things in the way: his boxers and her pajama bottoms and the tangled blanket.

And then they were struggling, squirming and twisting to shed their clothes and the blanket without breaking their kiss.

Somehow they succeeded. The last thing to go were her pajamas, and when she was finally free of them she wrapped her legs around Caleb's hips and tried to pull him down to her.

He was too strong.

"Protection," he gasped, his body rigid as he held himself a few inches away, his eyes wild as he looked down at her.

"IUD," she said, trying to make it into a sentence. "I have an IUD." She dug her heels into his lower back and her nails into the thick muscles between his shoulder blades, fierce and desperate and savage.

But she might have been a kitten swatting at a big dog for all the good it did. Caleb stayed exactly where he was, his arms on either side of her shoulders as he looked into her eyes.

Something in his expression made her go still.

And then, slowly, he found her center and slid inside.

He was so big it should have hurt, but she was so wet it didn't. She stared up at him and tried to breathe, every muscle in her body yearning for him even as their bodies joined.

His face was tense with an ecstasy she'd never seen in another human being. Inch by inch he sank into her, and it felt so good and so perfect and so exactly what she wanted that she felt the sting of tears in her nose and her throat and behind her eyes.

He stopped moving. "Am I hurting you?"

"No. No."

"Then why are you crying?"

"Because you feel so good."

He rested his forehead against hers.

"Say that again," he whispered, and she felt the breath of his words on her lips.

"You feel so good."

He was trembling. She could feel the tremors running through both their bodies.

"Are you all right?"

He nodded. "I'm just . . . trying not to move. I'm afraid I'm going to come." He raised his head again and looked her in the eyes. "I don't want to come yet. I want this to last forever."

Something pierced her heart—a lance of sweetness and pain.

"Nothing lasts forever," she said.

She arched her back to bring them closer, and he groaned.

When he pulled out and thrust back in, the pleasure tightened in her belly, and when he did it again, and again, she felt herself losing control.

When the explosion crashed over her, she cried out, and in that instant she wanted the same thing Caleb did.

She wanted this moment to last forever.

But even in the grip of ecstasy, she knew that it wouldn't.

Chapter Twelve

Caleb woke up like he always did: completely. He'd never understood people who woke up in stages, yawning and stretching and stumbling into the day. Ever since he was a kid, Caleb had gone from asleep to awake in the blink of an eye.

It took him only a second to remember where he was . . . and who he was with.

He was lying on his back in Jane's bed. He turned his head, and there she was: curled up facing him, her eyes closed and one hand tucked under her cheek, her long brown hair scattered on the white pillow like chestnut silk.

He watched her sleep for a long time. If he studied her face long enough, would he understand why she had such a hold on him?

It didn't make any sense. They weren't alike. They'd never had anything in common, except for Sam.

Now they didn't even have that.

It was a mystery. The kind of mystery that could make a man break every promise he'd ever made to himself, so he could follow the thread of it for the rest of his life.

Then Jane stirred and opened her eyes, and common sense came back with a dull thud.

He wasn't that kind of man. He wouldn't change his life to be with a woman.

Not even this woman.

As he read Jane's changing emotions—confusion, remembrance, awareness, uncertainty—he steeled himself to say the things that needed to be said.

Last night was a mistake. I'm sorry.

He felt his body stirring.

But please, can we do it again?

"Hey," Jane said, her voice soft.

He reached out and brushed her cheek with the back of his hand. "Hey."

Her skin was warm and rosy with sleep. He wanted to pull her into his arms and feel her naked body against his, but he forced himself to stay still. They lay like that for a long moment, just looking at each other.

He could gaze into Jane's eyes forever and never get to the end of her.

"Stay with me for Christmas."

He froze. "What?"

She smiled a little. "You don't have to look so panicked. I'm only talking about a couple of weeks."

I'm not panicking.

But how else would he describe the sudden tension in his muscles, the prick of adrenaline, his elevated heart rate?

He took a deep breath and let it out slowly. "I always spend Christmas alone."

"I know. I'm asking you not to this year."

"I'm leaving for Australia tomorrow."

She sighed. "I know that, too. Can't you change your ticket and fly out after New Year's?"

"You should go to your parents for the holidays," he said, avoiding her question. "That's the reason I came here yesterday."

He knew that was a mistake even before Jane sat up and stared at him.

"What are you talking about? What do my parents have to do with you coming here?"

The covers had fallen to her waist, and he tried not to look at her smooth, perfect breasts as he answered.

"Nina called me yesterday."

She slid down a little, pulling the covers up to her collarbone. "I see. And what did my mother have to say?"

"Your parents want you home for Christmas, and they'll buy you a new plane ticket." He paused. "You should go, Jane."

She looked away from him. "So that's why you stopped by. Because my mother asked you to."

"That's not the only reason."

"Then why didn't you come before? You've been in the city for two months, haven't you? You could have come by anytime."

"I might have, if you'd answered any of my phone calls or texts. But you didn't. It was pretty obvious you didn't want me anywhere near you."

She frowned a little, still looking away. Then she turned back to him.

"You're right. I'm sorry."

Jane's willingness to admit she was wrong was a rare quality, and it always took him by surprise.

"I'm sorry, too," he said after a moment. "It didn't matter that you weren't taking my calls. I should have come by anyway."

Her expression softened. "That's all right."

The strain between them eased, but that only made him aware of a different kind of tension.

Jane's comforter was thick, but he'd spent the night with her in his arms, and he knew what she looked like under it. For eight years, he'd only been able to imagine—and he had, even though he'd tried not to, and had felt guilty every time it happened.

He reached out for the comforter and gave a tug.

Jane's eyes widened in surprise, and her grip on the covers tightened.

His second tug was stronger, and the comforter ended up on the floor.

She was perfect. All smooth skin and slender curves, her nipples hardening at the sudden draft of cool air—and maybe something else.

"Caleb—"

He covered her body with his, and then he kissed her.

The feel of Jane beneath him brought out something primitive— more primitive than the instinct to make a fire against the cold, or to eat when he was hungry. He wanted to drown in her, to breathe her in like air.

For the first moment her body was stiff. But as he slid a hand into her hair and his thigh between her legs, he felt her soften. She moaned and arched up against him, kissing him with a passion that turned his bones to water.

But then, suddenly, she was pushing against his chest.

He rolled off her body and onto his side. "Did I hurt you?"

She shook her head, reaching for the sheet and using it to cover herself.

"No. But I don't want to do this."

Her face was flushed, her eyes dark and drugged with desire. He reached out and ran his palm down her body, one long stroke from her collarbone to her thighs, with only the sheet between his skin and hers.

"You sure about that?"

He could feel her quivering. His own body was rigid and aching, his heart pounding, his blood wild.

Jane closed her eyes and opened them again. "If you keep touching me, I'll do anything you want. You know that, Caleb. But I'm asking you to stop."

It felt like the hardest thing he'd ever done. But he pulled his hand away and shifted his weight, putting a few inches of space between them.

"What's going on, Jane?"

She sighed, and he couldn't tell if she was relieved or regretful.

"Will you stay with me for Christmas?"

He frowned. "We talked about that. Your parents want you home, and I'm flying to Australia tomorrow."

She was looking at him with those blue eyes, and he couldn't read her expression. "When are you coming back?"

His muscles tensed.

"I don't know," he muttered. "A few months, at least."

"And after that?"

"I don't know."

It was one of the things he and Sam had liked best about their business. They never planned too far ahead.

Jane nodded, as if his answer was what she'd been expecting. The energy between them shifted. She didn't move, at least not physically, but he could feel her pulling away.

A wave of anger went through him.

"I'm not leaving until tomorrow. Why can't we—"

"Make love until you have to leave for the airport?" She shook her head. "That really is your idea of the perfect relationship, isn't it?"

Another wave of anger. "When did we start talking about a relationship? I thought we were talking about here and now."

She smiled a little. "Sorry. That's the mistake every woman makes with you, isn't it? They sleep with you and start thinking about the future. They think they're different. Special."

His heart squeezed in his chest.

You are *different. You* are *special.*

How could she not know that? How could she have experienced last night and not know that?

Their connection wasn't just physical. He'd had physical chemistry with women before, and it had never felt like this. He'd shared more than his body with Jane last night.

For the first time, he let himself think about doing what she'd asked. He could change his plane ticket and stay here over the holidays—or even fly with her to LA to spend Christmas with her parents.

He rolled onto his back and closed his eyes.

To him, Christmas would always mean loss. Things falling apart. Over the years he'd learned to stop dreading the holidays, but that was only because of the tradition he'd started when he was eighteen. For the last twelve years, he'd spent the week between Christmas and New Year's hiking alone.

Once adventure trekking became his business, he'd had much less time by himself in the wilderness. This one week a year had become sacrosanct. He already had a solitary trek planned out for himself in Australia, before his first group expedition in January.

He could give it up this year, of course. He could sacrifice his Christmas tradition to be with Jane.

But it wouldn't end there, would it?

Once you started changing yourself for someone, you could never stop. He knew from watching his parents—and from his own dating experience—that it would never be enough. Your partner would expect you to change more and more of who you were. Eventually the sacrifices made you bitter, and you took it out on the other person. And that's when everything fell apart.

If he and Jane spent Christmas together, it would be the start of something—and he knew all too well how it would end. She lived here in New York, and he lived . . . nowhere. That wasn't a recipe for happily-ever-after.

And if any woman in the world deserved a happily-ever-after, it was Jane.

She was still trying to cope with Sam's death, which was probably why they'd ended up in bed last night. But once she began to heal, she'd be back to thinking about dream men and fairy tales and romantic gestures.

That wasn't him. If they tried to turn last night into something more, he'd let her down again and again. Then, after everything good between them had turned sour, they'd call it quits.

Jane's hand brushed against the side of his face.

"Hey," she said softly, and he opened his eyes.

"It's all right," she said. "I know last night was just last night. I know you're leaving, and I know you can't change your plane ticket. That's why I didn't want to make love again this morning. I'm not a masochist, and I'm not stupid."

He reached up and covered her hand with his, holding it against his cheek.

"You are stupid if you don't know you're special. If you don't know that last night was special."

It wasn't the kind of thing he usually said, and he sounded gruff and awkward saying it.

"I felt the same way," Jane said, pulling her hand back. "But I guess it's not enough."

After a moment she curled up on her side, facing him, her head resting on her folded arm. The sheet, caught partly under her body, stretched over the curve of her hip.

He didn't want to be having this conversation. He didn't want to be talking at all. He wanted to slide under that sheet with Jane and stay there until it was time to go to the airport. He wanted to make love to her again. He'd been like a teenager last night, desperate and lustful, unable to take his time. His plane didn't leave until tomorrow. There was no reason he couldn't spend today being the kind of lover Jane deserved.

Except she didn't want that.

She rolled onto her other side and sat up, keeping her back to him. She had the most perfect back he'd ever seen, graceful and beautiful, from her delicate shoulder blades to the incurve above her hips. He reached for her before he could stop himself, but she got up and went over to the closet.

She pulled open the door and grabbed a long-sleeved shirt, leaving the door open when she went to the bureau. As she pulled out a pair of sweatpants and started to dress, he looked back at the closet. Something on the shelf above the hanger rod had caught his eye.

"Will you go to LA for Christmas?" he asked abruptly.

She turned to face him again, her hands reaching up to braid her hair. "Probably not."

"I wish you wouldn't braid your hair," he almost growled.

She stared at him, her hands stilling for a moment. "Why?"

"I just . . . like it better down."

She stared at him a moment longer. Then, slowly and deliberately, she finished her braid.

His hands curled into fists. "Why won't you go to LA?"

"Because I don't want to."

"You'd rather stay here and wallow in your misery."

Her eyes narrowed. "I'm not wallowing. Sam only died two months ago."

He pointed at the closet. "You haven't scattered her ashes yet. I can see the urn right there. Is this how you're planning to spend Christmas? Alone in your apartment with that thing? If you won't go home to be with your family, at least do something worthwhile and scatter Sam's ashes the way she wanted."

She flinched as though he'd struck her. "You read the letter she left. She wanted me to climb some mountain in Maine, and it's the middle of winter. I'll go in the spring." She paused. "Or maybe the summer."

He couldn't stop himself from wading deeper into the quagmire.

"Or maybe you'll never scatter her ashes, because you can't let go. You blame yourself for Sam's death, even though you know how stupid that is. And you're punishing yourself. That's the real reason you won't go home for Christmas."

Jane took a step toward him. "Thank you so much for your keen insight." Her voice was shaking, and she paused to take a deep breath. "But what about you, Caleb?"

He was still in bed, the blanket covering his naked body from the hips down. Now he threw off the covers and strode into the living room.

Her voice followed him. "You think I'm staying here because of Sam. Well, I think you're leaving because of Sam."

He pulled on his boxers, his jeans, his T-shirt. Then he turned to face her. "What are you talking about?"

Jane had followed him as far as her bedroom doorway. She was standing there with her arms folded, leaning against the doorframe.

"Being in New York makes you think about her. Maybe being around me makes you think about her, too. That hurts, and so you're leaving. You're running away like you always do."

He sat on the couch to pull on his boots.

"I don't run away from things."

"Oh, really? Then answer me one question."

He looked at her. "What?"

"Why do you always spend Christmas alone?"

His jaw tightened. "That's none of your damn business."

"Then I'm none of your business."

"What the hell does that even mean?"

"You came here to save me, didn't you? Cleaning and cooking and . . ." Her mouth started to tremble, and she pressed her lips together a moment before she continued. "And all that other stuff. You came here and made me be alive again. But I'm not allowed to do that for you, am I? No one is."

His hands had clenched into fists without his realizing it. He forced himself to relax, and then he looked around for his jacket.

"Saying that proves you don't know me at all. I am alive, Jane. And unlike you, I try to live like it every single day."

He'd put his jacket in the closet by the front door. He grabbed it off the hanger and pulled it on, and then there was nothing keeping him from leaving.

Jane was still standing in the doorway to her bedroom. She looked small and forlorn and defiant, and all his anger faded away.

He took a step toward her. "I'm sorry." He dragged a hand through his hair. "Really sorry."

She looked at him for a long moment. "Stay with me for Christmas, Caleb."

He glanced around her apartment. "You're not exactly ready for the holidays."

One corner of her mouth lifted, and he realized with a pang that it was the first time he'd seen her smile since Sam died.

"I have seasonal underwear," she said, and paused. "We could get ready together. Buy a tree, decorate, shop for presents."

He had a sudden image of what it would be like to celebrate Christmas with Jane.

It would be heaven.

For the last twelve years, he'd spent Christmas alone. Was Jane right? Was it finally time for a change?

The cold clutch of panic gripped his heart and stopped his breath.

Jane was still dealing with her sister's death. If he was going to face old pain and old demons, this was the worst time to do it.

Or maybe the truth was that he'd never do it.

The moment was over. And the funny thing was, Jane realized it before he did.

"It's okay," she said, sliding her hands into her pockets. "Maybe next year."

It's what she and Sam used to say every December when he turned down their annual holiday invitation.

Only this time, Jane didn't have Sam beside her.

"There's something I want for Christmas," he said abruptly.

She raised her eyebrows. "You're asking me for a present? I don't think you've ever done that before. What is it?"

"I want you to go home for the holidays. I want you to be with your family."

He expected her to argue or to simply say no. But then she shrugged.

A Jane Finch shrug. He wondered, like he always did, what she wasn't saying.

"Okay," she said.

He stared at her. "Really?"

"Really."

"You'll go home for Christmas."

"I'll go home for Christmas."

"Are you just saying that to get me to leave?"

She rolled her eyes. "No."

"You should call your parents right away so they can get the ticket."

"They already bought me one ticket. I'll buy this one."

"Last minute for the holidays? It'll be expensive as hell."

"I can afford it. I haven't spent much money the last couple of months."

"Do you want me to—"

"No. I don't need your help, Caleb. I can manage." She paused. "Have a good trip, okay?" She took a step toward him, and he saw the muscles of her throat move as she swallowed. "Stay safe, Caleb. I . . ." She shook her head. "Stay safe."

He didn't want to leave her. He felt it in his heart, his gut, every cell in his body.

"You too," he said gruffly.

He stood there another moment, wanting to stay, wanting to go, wanting Sam to walk in and ask what the hell was wrong with the two of them.

Then, with an effort, he turned the knob and left.

Chapter Thirteen

January was hard, and February wasn't much easier. March was a little better. Jane was at the bookstore a lot, but she didn't want to cut her employees' hours, so she came up with a way to keep everyone busy.

She owned the second floor of her building, but she'd never used it for anything but storage. You had to get to those rooms from a separate entrance, so it didn't make sense to expand the bookstore up there.

Now, finally, she thought of a way to use that space.

In one of the quiet back rooms she set up writing desks; in another she put easels and her grandmother's old pottery wheel. In the big sun-drenched front room with the beautiful wooden floors, she put up a ballet barre on one wall and mirrors on the other. In the small room at the top of the stairs she put a conference table and chairs for writers' groups or play readings or anything else people might want it for.

Her investment was minimal, so she could afford to keep her prices low. Artists and dancers could rent studio space. Writers could rent a desk for an hour or a day.

"But what are you getting out of this?" Kiki asked, skeptical of the new project.

"Money."

"Not very much."

"More than I thought when we started. We're getting pretty popular."

"You don't care about the money. What else are you getting from this?"

Jane shrugged. "Company I don't have to talk to."

Kiki was an extrovert, so she didn't really understand the appeal. But Jane found comfort in being around people she didn't have to interact with, especially people who were reading or writing or painting. The quiet in the writing room and art studio felt rich and warm, not cold and empty like the silence in her apartment.

Of course, that wasn't the only reason her apartment felt cold.

Caleb had spent a night there, and now he was gone.

Weeks went by before she could sleep at night without dreaming of him, or lying awake remembering the heat of his skin, the weight of his body, the look in his eyes as he sank into her.

The difference between Caleb and other men wasn't on a continuum. It wasn't like her last boyfriend was a six and Caleb was a ten. It was more like everything else had been in two dimensions, and her night with Caleb had been in three.

It had been a whole other world.

But it wouldn't do her any good to remember that night. She'd had a few texts from Caleb, and she'd sent a few to him, but the one time he'd called—on her birthday, in February—had felt stilted, and they hadn't talked since.

It was getting harder to believe that their one night of passionate, fevered intensity had been real.

The one thing she was sure of was that it would never be repeated.

He was in Australia, and she was here. And when he wasn't in Australia anymore, he still wouldn't be here.

He'd never be here.

But she was, and she was doing her best to act like it.

She split her time between the bookstore and what she'd started calling the artists' colony. One unexpected—but welcome—side effect of the new venture was that her store had become very popular with aspiring writers, who, it turned out, bought a lot of books. That meant she could give Felicia and Kiki as many hours as they wanted, and business was thriving.

She'd found a delicate balance for herself, between busyness and reflection, time alone and time with people, thinking about Sam and Caleb and not thinking about them. She knew she was still in danger of slipping back into depression, but she hadn't realized anyone else knew it until the day she came into the shop and heard her employees arguing.

"I'm going to burn it," said Felicia.

"It's not yours, and destroying mail is a felony." That was Kiki.

"This isn't mail. It's not stamped."

"It's a letter, and it doesn't have anything to do with you."

"The heck it doesn't. You remember what she was like at Christmas, and you know how good she's been lately. Do you really want to give her this thing and take a chance that—"

Jane stepped into view. "Take a chance that what?"

The two of them stared at her, and Felicia, holding a letter in her hands, flushed bright red from her neck to her ears.

"It's nothing. Just a—"

Kiki snatched it away and held it out to Jane.

"It's a letter for Sam. We found it wedged behind a drawer when we were cleaning."

Jane's hand closed over the envelope. She recognized it instantly, and she wished for a moment that Felicia had won the argument and burned it.

She wasn't afraid of remembering her sister anymore, but she was afraid of remembering the handsome stranger who'd fallen in love with her. She was afraid of remembering her resentment and jealousy, and the question she'd asked herself over and over again last Christmas.

Could she have made Sam stay in the city by telling her about Dan?

Logic said no, but her heart had said *maybe*, and *what if*, and a hundred other agonizing things.

She took a deep breath and looked up at Kiki and Felicia, and the concern on their faces was like a warm fire on a cold day.

Her face relaxed into a smile. "It's all right," she said. "Thanks for worrying about me, though. I'll be upstairs, okay?"

She took the letter with her and walked slowly up to the second floor, sitting at one of the empty writing desks. It was still early, and the room was only half-full. In the desk nearest her, a young woman sat with a dreamy look on her face and a laptop open in front of her.

Jane opened the letter and laid it on the desk.

Dear Samantha,

We don't know each other yet, so this letter might seem crazy to you. But from the moment I first saw you in your sister's bookshop, something happened to me. It was as though all the light in the universe was shining through you, and I wanted to follow wherever you might lead.

Jane has told me a little about you, and I know you loved *Anne of Green Gables* when you were a little girl. If you feel like taking a chance on a man who fell in love with you at first sight, I have a proposition.

Prince Edward Island is my home. If you happen to be single when spring arrives, I hope you'll come meet me at the Lake of Shining Waters. There's a bridge at one end any local will direct you to, and I will be there at sunset on May 1.

Yours in hope,
Daniel Smith

Jane sat and stared at the letter for a long time. Then she folded it up, put it back in the envelope, and started to think.

He was going to be at the Lake of Shining Waters on May 1, waiting for a woman who would never come. And it was her fault. She'd created an imaginary Sam for him to fall in love with, and now that lie was out there in the world.

She'd told Dan that Samantha loved *Anne of Green Gables*. The book was set on Prince Edward Island in Canada, where, apparently, Dan actually lived. That must have made him feel even more connected to the woman she'd described.

The Lake of Shining Waters was a place from the book, and apparently it also existed in real life. So when Dan wanted to invite Sam to a romantic meeting, he'd chosen a spot he thought would be meaningful to them both.

And it would have been . . . if she were the one Dan had written the letter to. She couldn't think of anything more romantic than meeting a man at the place where Anne Shirley had once been rescued by handsome, dashing Gilbert Blythe.

But Dan hadn't written to her. He'd written to Sam.

Jane put her head in her hands.

There was a chapter in *Anne of Green Gables* called "A Good Imagination Gone Wrong," about how Anne's vivid tales of ghosts and ghouls had gotten her in trouble. As a person with a colorful imagination of her own, Jane sympathized. But except for making her a little forgetful now and then—the occasional missed subway stop or dentist appointment—her own imagination had never seemed like a liability.

Now it did. She'd messed up, and she had to fix it. Dan deserved the truth, and Sam deserved to be remembered for who she had really been.

She took a deep breath, and then she went back downstairs.

"I need to go to Canada for a few days," she said to Kiki and Felicia. "Can you guys handle the store?" She paused. "Also, do either of you know where I can go to get a passport?"

Kiki and Felicia looked at each other and then back at her.

"Are you feeling all right, Jane?" Kiki asked cautiously.

"Of course I'm all right. I just need to take a trip."

Felicia rested her elbows on the counter and leaned forward. "Now, I ask you. If one of us suddenly announced we had to go to Canada immediately, wouldn't you think that was weird?"

"I don't need to go immediately. I just need to be there on May 1."

Kiki looked skeptical. "That's barely enough time to get a passport."

"Well, that's good to know. See? That's why I asked you guys. You both like to travel. You know things I don't know."

"What's happening on May 1?" Felicia asked. "Something to do with that letter?"

Jane squeezed it in her hand. "An appointment Sam won't be able to keep."

"Sam was supposed to meet someone in Canada on May 1?"

She nodded. "So I'm going instead."

Kiki leaned toward her. "This isn't sounding any less crazy. Can't you explain what—"

"No. I don't want to talk about it. I just need to plan the trip."

Kiki and Felicia looked at each other again. Felicia raised her eyebrows, and Kiki shrugged.

"Well, the first thing you need to do is apply for a passport. You can have it expedited, but that'll cost you extra."

Jane nodded. "Okay, I'll start there." She took a deep breath. "What do I have to do?"

❖ ❖ ❖

The ridges and ranges of western Australia were 350 million years old. A man who loved wild places could spend years here, exploring the largest expanse of outback in the country. Between the ancient beauty of the land and the cattle ranches and rodeos, Caleb should have felt as comfortable here as any place on earth.

He was on horseback, watching the sun set over a spectacular river gorge. The wild splendor of the landscape should have lifted his spirits. But all he could think about was how much Sam would have loved it here—and what Jane would say if he could ever get her out of New York and into a scene like this.

He turned away from the sunset and rode slowly back to the ranch where he was staying. He'd met the owner on a trek years ago and was taking him up on an offer of free room and board in exchange for his help with the animals—cattle as well as horses. It was an ideal arrangement: a couple of weeks working on the ranch, followed by a couple of weeks leading expeditions in the outback.

It should have been perfect.

His horse was a mare called Restless, and every time he saddled her up he remembered something Sam had said to him once.

"You're the most restless man I've ever known."

He missed her every day, almost every hour. He missed her humor and strength, her unwavering friendship, her hunger for life.

She'd been his partner and his best friend. And yet, whenever she'd offered him opportunities to open up to her about the scars of his childhood, he'd always declined.

He'd told himself it was because he was a private man. But maybe what Jane had said was closer to the truth.

You're running away like you always do.

He'd run as far from both sisters as he could. He was half a world away from Sam's ashes and half a world away from Jane. Australia should have been far enough to escape the pain of Sam's absence and to break Jane's hold on his heart.

Instead, both were stronger than ever.

He'd accused Jane of not dealing with Sam's death, but he hadn't, either. It still felt like an open wound. The pain of it made him think of other, older wounds . . . the ones he thought he'd left behind years ago.

His mother, his father, Sam. He'd loved them, and they'd died or left. And instead of healing, their absence was an ache in his heart that never got better.

Jane's absence hurt in a different way.

His Christmas hike, which he always made challenging enough to occupy his full attention, had been dull and stale this year. His thoughts kept turning to Jane, missing Jane, wanting Jane, until he finally acknowledged the truth.

He should have stayed with her for the holidays.

It was impossible to imagine them as a couple—they were too different, and their lives would never mesh. She didn't belong in the wilderness with him, and she deserved better than a long-distance relationship.

But he'd give anything, now, to have had one more night with her. And an entire week? It would have been paradise. The kind of memory that could have kept him warm on cold nights and reminded him that his heart—and other body parts—were alive and well.

But he'd passed up that chance, choosing his solitary Christmas tradition over time with Jane. And he'd regret that decision for a long time to come.

He'd called her on her birthday, and at the sound of her voice he'd gotten tongue-tied, like a thirteen-year-old boy talking to his first crush. Then he'd pulled himself together and overcompensated, trying to go back to the banter they'd once shared. That effort had fallen flat.

The weight of what he'd really wanted to say had been unbearable. *I miss you. I think about you. Do you think about me?*

He hadn't said any of that, of course. But after they'd hung up, he'd almost driven to the airport to get on a plane bound for New York.

The only thing that stopped him was not knowing how Jane would react. He couldn't stand the idea that she might send him away—or worse, feel sorry for him. Maybe it was just masculine pride, but he wasn't willing to risk her rejection.

Two months had gone by since then. He and Jane had texted a few times, but they hadn't spoken on the phone since her birthday. The more time went by without them talking, the less likely it seemed that they could ever go back to the way things had been before Sam's death . . . much less that their one incredible night together would ever be repeated.

Visa requirements would send him back to the States soon, before he could return to Australia for a few more months. His brother and aunt were lobbying for him to come to Colorado, and he supposed that made the most sense.

More sense than going to New York.

The last rays of the setting sun turned the landscape golden. He slowed Restless to a walk as they neared the ranch, giving her time to cool down before they reached the stable.

Once inside, he spent longer than usual grooming her. He found a horse's stall, as always, a peaceful place to be.

If only he could find that same peace within himself.

As he walked from the stables to the outbuilding where he was living, his phone vibrated in his pocket. He pulled it out and saw Kiki's name on the screen.

They'd exchanged numbers last November, when they'd both been worried about Jane. Why would she be calling now?

Ten minutes later, he knew the answer.

Chapter Fourteen

A few days after reading Dan's letter, Jane was at the register ringing up a new mystery for Alicia when the older woman looked over her shoulder and smiled.

"I know that look," Jane said, sliding Alicia's bag across the counter. "Did you spot Colin Firth driving by in a taxi?"

Alicia shook her head. "Not Colin Firth. That cowboy. The one who knows you."

Jane froze. She stared at Alicia, unable to turn her head, as every one of the fine hairs at the back of her neck stood up.

It couldn't be. They'd exchanged texts a few weeks ago—*Hi, how's it going, everything's fine, how about you*—and Caleb hadn't said anything about coming to New York. Nothing like *By the way, I'm coming to town soon. How about dinner?*

She still couldn't move. She felt like she was in one of those dreams where you need to run, but your feet are stuck in cement.

"Hello, darlin'."

The sound of his voice released her from her strange paralysis, and she whirled to face him.

She was vaguely aware that Alicia had taken her bag and discreetly left the store, leaving them alone.

He hadn't changed. His tan might have been a little deeper and his hair a touch lighter, but his hazel eyes and his lazy grin and his Stetson were still exactly the same. In spite of herself, she remembered the sensations she'd relived so many times since Christmas—the heat of his skin, the weight of his body.

The memories whipped color into her cheeks. Her hands clenched into fists. When she spoke, her voice was trembling.

"What kind of person flies in from freaking Australia without letting people know? Why didn't you tell me you were coming?"

He cocked his head to the side. "Well, darlin'—"

"Don't call me that." She reached out, snatched his hat off, and slapped it on the counter. "What are you doing here, Caleb?"

Without the hat, his eyes were a little easier to read. The dominant emotion seemed to be relief.

Why did he look relieved?

"I heard you were planning a trip to Canada," he said.

"So? What business is that of yours?" Something else occurred to her. "Wait a minute. Who told you I was going to Canada?"

"Well . . ."

She reached a rapid conclusion. "Oh my God. It had to be Kiki or Felicia. You asked one of them to spy on me, didn't you?"

"Well . . ."

She didn't let him finish. "I can't believe this. You had someone keeping an eye on me."

"If you just—"

"You couldn't be bothered to call or visit, but you asked one of my employees to report to you about my—what, exactly? My mental state?"

"Jane—"

"What do you have to say for yourself?"

"Not much, if you won't let me finish a sentence."

She slapped both hands on the counter and glared at him. "Fine. Go ahead and finish one."

There was a short silence.

"I didn't ask Kiki to keep an eye on you. She had my number from last fall, when we were worried about you. She got in touch with me a few days ago and said . . ."

"Yes? What did she say? That I'm going to Canada, so I must be out of my mind?"

He looked at her for a moment. Then he reached out and covered her hands with his, and his touch sent a wave of longing through her that she was terrified he'd see.

She snatched her hands away. "Was that it? You were worried I was going crazy or something?"

"No, and neither was Kiki. She was just concerned about you charging off to another country to meet the man who wrote that letter. She thought . . ."

"What? What did she think?"

"That you might have some, ah, unresolved grief about Sam, and that this trip of yours might not be the healthiest way to deal with it."

She frowned. "Since when do you talk like a psychologist?"

One corner of his mouth rose. "Those aren't my words, they're Kiki's. But I thought she might have a point."

She folded her arms. "You thought she might have a point. So instead of calling, you hopped on a plane and came halfway round the world to see me?"

"I needed to come back soon anyway. Visa requirements."

That caused a pang. "You could have told me that, too. Like, say, a few weeks ago, when we were texting."

"I wasn't planning to come to New York. I was going to Colorado, but then I heard from Kiki and—"

"You decided to drop by and check on me? How sweet."

He had to come back to the United States, but he hadn't been planning to come to New York. Not until Kiki told him she was worried did he take the trouble to come and see her.

The knowledge hurt more than she would have expected. More than she would ever let him know.

It was obvious their one night together hadn't meant much to him after all.

He didn't think of her as a lover. He still thought of her as Sam's kid sister, someone who needed to be protected.

All those hours she'd lain awake, reliving that night, seemed really stupid now.

"Jane."

He reached out and grabbed her hand again, but this time his touch wasn't gentle.

Just like that she was in her apartment again. Caleb was holding her in a grip like iron, and there was hunger in his eyes.

But there wasn't hunger in his eyes now. Only concern.

"How I got here doesn't matter," he said. "I'm here, and yeah, I'm worried about you. I don't think you're crazy, but I do think you're making some bad decisions."

She tugged on the wrist he held, and unlike that night at her apartment, he let her go.

"My decision making is fine, thank you very much."

"Then prove it to me. Let me buy you dinner tonight, and you can tell me all about this trip of yours."

"I don't have to prove anything to you."

"True," he said, taking his hat from the counter and putting it back on. "But if you don't have dinner with me, I'll call your parents and tell them how concerned Kiki and I are about you."

Her eyes widened. "You wouldn't."

"I would."

"My mother will call me nonstop. My father will send me long worried emails. One of them will fly out here. Maybe both of them."

"Yep."

She took a deep breath. "I didn't realize you'd actually resort to blackmail."

"Well, darlin', now you know. I'll meet you at that barbecue place in your neighborhood at eight o'clock." He tipped his hat and winked at her. "Till then, ma'am."

Before she could think of a retort, he was out the door and gone.

◆ ◆ ◆

Caleb made it around the corner before he had to stop and lean against the brick wall of the building beside him.

Sam had predicted once he'd fall hard someday. He'd told her she was crazy, and she'd insisted he was the type who'd go all in for the right woman.

She may have been right about that. But if she'd known the right woman was her own kid sister, she wouldn't have been so damn gleeful about it.

Because Sam had also understood that he was addicted to travel. She'd said that if he ever did fall for someone, she hoped to God it would be another adventurer.

But his job wasn't the only reason he and Jane couldn't be together. Of course Sam could imagine him being with a soul mate—she'd never known that a part of him was broken, for the very good reason that he'd structured his life so no one would find out. If he was the kind of man who could share his life with someone—really share his life—then he would have stayed with Jane last Christmas.

But he hadn't stayed.

So yeah, maybe he'd fallen for Jane. But he didn't have what it would take to make her happy.

In fact, he was probably the worst thing that could ever happen to her. And judging by her reaction just now, she knew it.

It had been stupid to think she might be happy to see him—especially if he showed up unexpectedly. A part of him had hoped that in the first moment of surprise she might betray some of what he felt for her.

She hadn't.

There was no future for them, and no present, either.

Which meant he was left with one night to remember. One night that would haunt him like a beloved ghost for the rest of his life.

But before he left again, he had a job to do. Sam had trusted him to look after her little sister, and he wasn't going to let her down.

◆　◆　◆

He was at the barbecue joint half an hour early, but he didn't order a beer. He didn't want any alcohol in his system, anything that might make him susceptible to the fierce urgency he felt whenever he was around Jane, the need to throw her over his shoulder and carry her off to his cave.

He needed a fully sober brain to override his body.

Jane was early, too. She came in at ten minutes to eight, looked around, and spotted him at the corner booth he'd snagged.

"Hi," she said, sliding in across from him.

"Hi."

The waitress appeared before they could say anything else. "Can I get you a drink?"

"Um . . . a Diet Coke?"

"Sure thing. Are you two ready to order, or do you need a minute?"

Jane glanced at the menu in front of her, but she didn't open it. "I'll just have a salad."

She looked a little thinner since the last time he'd seen her, and the need to stuff her full of high-calorie food overrode the voice in his head telling him not to push his luck.

"This is a barbecue place," he said. "You should get ribs."

She glared at him. "Just a salad," she said to the waitress.

His hand curled into a fist on his thigh. "I'll take a full slab of ribs, beans, slaw, and cornbread."

"Sure thing," the waitress said, flashing him a smile before leaving.

Jane was still glaring at him.

"What?" he asked, defensively.

"Did you get her number yet?"

"Whose number? What the hell are you talking about?"

"The waitress. The one flirting with you."

"Jesus." He took off his hat, dragged a hand through his hair, and put the hat back on. "I didn't even notice her. Can we talk about Canada, please?"

She still didn't look happy. But she shrugged, reached into the quilted bag she'd put on the seat beside her, and pulled out a letter.

"Here," she said, handing it to him. "This is why I'm going to Canada."

He read it through once. Then he read it again.

He handed it back to her. "You have to be kidding me."

"What does that mean?" she asked, slipping the letter back in her purse.

"You're going to Canada to meet this bullshit artist? Why?"

For a moment he thought she'd walk out on him. He could see her thinking about it. But then the waitress came with her Diet Coke, and the moment was over.

She took a sip of her drink. "This bullshit artist, as you call him, is actually capable of falling in love."

The obvious implication being that he wasn't.

Jane went on. "He's going to be there at sunset on May 1, waiting for a woman who will never come. And it's my fault."

"So write him a letter or something. You don't have to go all the way to Canada."

"I don't have his address or contact information. I have to go in person." She bit her lip. "Don't you understand? I didn't tell him the truth about Sam. I didn't tell him who she really was. I can't leave things like that, knowing that lie is in the world. I have to make it right."

He shook his head. "You're torturing yourself for nothing. I'll bet you a thousand dollars Horn-Rims won't be on that damn bridge. I know his type. He's got some kind of pathetic romantic fantasy going with some other woman by now, Jane. I promise you that."

She leaned forward, her eyes narrowing, and he prepared himself to be yelled at.

But she didn't yell. She pressed her lips tightly together, sat back, and fished around in her purse again. Then started to write, keeping the pen and paper out of sight.

After a moment, she slapped something down on the table between them.

A check made out to him for $1,000.

"It's a bet," she said.

He looked down at the check and back up at her. "You're not serious."

"Yes, I am."

Her eyes were glittering, and he knew if they really got into it things would get ugly.

Then something occurred to him.

"Fine."

She blinked, and he realized with satisfaction that the last thing she'd expected was for him to call her bluff.

"But since it's a bet, I have a right to proof."

She was still trying to assess this new twist. "Proof?"

"How will I know if Horn-Rims was really on the bridge when he said he'd be? You could lie and say he was, but—"

Her eyes narrowed and fire looked imminent once again. "You think I'd lie about it? You think I'd—"

"I don't have to think anything. I'd rather know for sure."

"And how exactly do you expect to—"

"I'm going with you."

She blinked again, and the expression on her face was worth being back in New York.

"What do you mean, you're going with me?"

"I mean I'm taking you to Canada." He paused. "How are you planning to get there, anyway? I looked it up online, and most people drive across the Confederation Bridge from New Brunswick and use their own cars to get around the island. Seems like a simple plan, with one obvious problem." He cocked his head to the side. "You don't have a car or a driver's license."

She flushed. "I live in New York! Lots of people in the city don't drive."

"There's a whole world out there to explore, you know. New York isn't actually the center of the universe."

"I know that! I—" She shook her head sharply. "Okay, not the point. The point is, I can take a plane to the Charlottetown airport."

"And then what? Get around by taxi? Sounds inconvenient and expensive. Wouldn't it make more sense to have your own transportation?"

"Well, sure, but—"

"Now you do." He folded his arms. "Me."

She folded her arms, too. "You're the last person in the world I want to take a sixteen-hour car ride with."

That stung a little. "Too bad. I have a right to oversee my bet." He paused. "Unless you decide to cancel the trip altogether. You'd be off the hook then."

"You can't bully me into cancelling."

"I'm not bullying you, damn it!"

Her lips twitched a little. It wasn't much, just the hint of a smile, but it eased some of the tension between them.

He unfolded his arms, rested his forearms on the table, and clasped his hands. "Tell me why this is so important to you. Please, Jane. I really want to know."

She looked away for a moment, her expression uncertain. He just waited, still and silent, hoping the waitress wouldn't pick this moment to arrive with their food.

Finally Jane looked back at him. "Because he loved Sam. Or at least he thought he did."

Bullshit, he wanted to say, but for once he kept his stupid mouth shut.

After a moment she went on. "I thought you'd see it, too, once you read his letter. I know you don't believe in love at first sight, but you read how he described her." She took a breath. "'It was as though all the light in the universe was shining through you.'"

She put her elbows on the table and her head in her hands, and he wanted to reach out for her so bad it hurt.

But he stayed still, and a minute later she looked up. Her eyes were dry, but they were bright.

"How can you say he's full of shit after reading that? It's the most perfect description of Sam I've ever heard."

His heart twisted in his chest. "She wasn't an angel or a saint." His throat felt tight and his voice was gruff, and he grabbed his water glass to take a sip.

"I never said she was. But she was so . . ." Her hands lifted, sketching shapes in the air. "So bright. You know she was, Caleb. She was full of life, full of joy. Full of light."

The tightness in his throat spread to his chest, making it hard to draw a deep breath. His eyes stung, and he fought so hard to keep tears from forming that he almost missed Jane's next words.

"I know I screwed everything up by lying to him, but it didn't stop him from seeing into Sam's heart. Her essence. Don't you see? He saw something in her worth loving. Something bright and beautiful. And it wasn't just her physical beauty."

"You think he saw into her soul or something?"

He wasn't able to hide his skepticism.

"I don't know," she said. "But it's possible." She leaned forward. "And I'm not going to let him go to that bridge and wait for her and wonder why she didn't come. I'm going to meet him, and I'm going to tell him I lied about her loving books and wanting to be a writer and all that stuff, but that the Sam he fell for was the real Sam. I'm going to tell him who she was and that he was right to love her."

He could deal with feisty Jane and pissed off Jane and sarcastic Jane. But when she was like this, all earnest and intense and sincere, she was too much for him.

"All right, fine. But I'm still coming with you."

"But *why*? And don't tell me it's about the stupid bet."

Jane thought she could find a way through her pain by going somewhere else, and that was something Caleb understood. But if Jane was finally going to leave this city on an actual journey, he would damn well make sure she accomplished something worthwhile.

"Because there's one important thing you're going to do on this trip, and it isn't meeting Horn-Rims at the Lake of Shining Waters. Whatever the hell that is."

"What important thing? What are you talking about?"

"I'm talking about scattering your sister's ashes."

Chapter Fifteen

Jane put her passport in the front pocket of her suitcase because it zipped and her purse didn't, and she thought it would be safer there. But what if something happened to her suitcase? Shouldn't she keep her passport with her at all times?

Of course she was going to Canada, not China or the Middle East. She spoke the language, and it was a friendly government. But still.

She checked the time. Caleb would be here in twenty minutes.

That's what she was really nervous about. Not losing her passport, but being in a car with Caleb for two days.

And if that wasn't enough, they also had to haul a ceramic urn to the top of a mountain in Maine. Owl Mountain, to be specific. Sam had been very clear about that in the letter they'd found with her will and other papers.

"How do you know I haven't already done it?" she'd asked Caleb that night at dinner.

"I'll bet you ten thousand dollars you haven't."

"You'd actually make a bet about my sister's mortal remains?"

He'd grinned at her. "Sam loved a good bet, as you very well know. She'd approve. What she wouldn't approve of is you keeping her in the back of a closet. I'm surprised you haven't heard a little voice from in there singing 'Don't Fence Me In.'"

She'd laughed in spite of herself and then felt horrible for laughing. How could she find anything about her sister's ashes funny?

"Hey," Caleb had said, looking at her with that way he had—his way of making it seem like everything would be all right. "Sam would've loved that joke, and she would've loved that you laughed at it." He'd paused. "And she'll love that you're going to scatter her ashes from a mountaintop, just like she wanted."

And now here she was, about to take a thousand-mile journey with a man she lusted after but would never have, to scatter Sam's ashes from the top of a mountain she was terrified to climb, all so she could meet a man she didn't know to tell him the woman he'd fallen in love with was dead.

It sounded like a recipe for disaster.

She wished she hadn't let Caleb talk her into the hiking thing. Yes, she owed it to Sam—but there was no rush, was there? She'd been planning to wait until summer. If not this year, then next. Or even two years.

She opened her closet door and looked up. There it was, tucked away at the back of the shelf: the gray ceramic urn her parents had chosen to hold Sam's ashes.

She was afraid to just reach up and grab it. What if it fell?

With morbid images of ashes on the bedroom floor filling her mind, she dragged a chair over and climbed up on it, closing her hands carefully around the urn and hefting its weight for a moment before—

The chair wobbled, and she had a split second to realize she was going down before she did.

She landed on her butt with the urn in her lap. It was cradled in her arms and she was hunched over it, protecting it with her body the way she would have protected a child in a fall.

It was fine. The lid was still on, and everything was fine.

She set the urn carefully on the floor beside her. Then she got to her feet, a little shaky, and took a deep breath.

And then, suddenly, she started to laugh.

She'd been worried about riding in a car beside Caleb Bryce, the human match to the gasoline of her sex drive. But she'd forgotten that she'd be travelling with the world's best mood-killer.

A ceramic pot full of human remains.

It felt good to laugh. And this time, she knew that what Caleb had said the other night was true: Sam had loved to laugh, and to make other people laugh, and she would have loved hearing her sister laugh now.

Twenty minutes later, she met Caleb at the door with the urn in her arms and her suitcase beside her.

He raised his eyebrows at the burden she carried. "I guess I'll carry this down, then," he said, picking up her suitcase and waiting for her to lock her apartment and precede him down the stairs.

"You seem surprised," she commented, standing on the sidewalk as he popped the trunk of his rental car—a dark blue four-door sedan. He put her suitcase in beside an old, beat-up pack.

"I guess I thought you'd have the urn in a box or a bag or something," he said. "Do you think it'll be safe in here?" he asked, shifting things in the trunk experimentally. "I guess we could wedge it in with—"

"No," she said firmly. "I want it in the back seat."

He raised his eyebrows again, but he closed the trunk and opened the rear passenger side door for her before going around to the driver's side.

She set the urn down on the butter-soft leather. For a moment she studied it, a glazed ceramic pot with white seagulls painted on a gray background, resting like a squat, rotund passenger on the seat behind hers. Then, on impulse, she pulled the seat belt around it and hooked it in.

"That looks really weird," Caleb commented, watching her in the rearview mirror.

"This whole trip is weird," she said as she slid into the front seat and buckled her own seat belt.

"Scattering your sister's ashes according to her wishes is not weird. Traveling with them in the back seat is a little weird. Going to meet a total stranger on a bridge in Canada is extremely weird."

They pulled away from the curb, and the early-morning sun was directly in their eyes for a moment. Jane blinked and pulled down the visor.

"I respectfully disagree, but I'm not going to fight about it."

"Well, that's a nice change." Caleb reached for the knobs on the radio and fiddled for a moment, but Jane swatted his hand away and pulled out her phone, plugging it into the port on the dash.

"You've got a playlist?" he asked.

"Not exactly."

"What, then?"

"You'll see," she said, opening her audiobook app and then settling back in her seat.

A female voice with perfect enunciation came through the speakers. "*Anne of Green Gables*, by L. M. Montgomery."

Caleb looked at her sideways. "You're kidding me."

"Nope."

"You're going to make me listen to a kids' book."

"Yep."

"A kids' book for girls."

"Yep."

"*Chapter one. Mrs. Rachel Lynde is surprised.*"

He sighed as he pulled up at a red light. "How long is this thing?"

She squinted at her phone screen. "Ten hours."

"Jesus."

She grinned at him. "Don't worry, you'll love it. Everyone does."

"I won't."

"Want to bet?"

"Hell yeah. How much?"

"Loser buys dinner tonight."

"Deal."

◆　◆　◆

He ended up hooked on the damn thing.

He didn't pay much attention to the first chapter. But when Matthew Cuthbert showed up at the train station to meet the orphan boy he and his sister were expecting and found scrawny, red-haired Anne Shirley there instead, he started to listen. And when Matthew and Marilla were deciding whether to keep her or send her back, he actually paused the audio at a tollbooth so he wouldn't miss anything.

It made the time seem to fly by.

Jane looked smug when he suggested they stop at a drive-through for lunch so they could eat in the car and keep listening. On their way through Massachusetts, Gilbert Blythe teased Anne in school by calling her "carrots," and she cracked her slate over his head. Crossing the border into New Hampshire, Anne accidentally made her friend Diana drunk by giving her currant wine instead of raspberry cordial. By the time they reached Maine, Anne had flavored a cake with anodyne liniment instead of vanilla.

"What the hell is anodyne liniment?" he asked, and Jane Googled it.

"It's an old remedy for pain relief. Let's see. It was considered good for coughs, colds, colic, asthmatic distress, bronchial colds, nasal catarrh, cholera morbus, cramps, diarrhea, bruises, common sore throat, burns and scalds, chaps and chafing, chilblains, frost bites, muscular rheumatism, soreness, sprains, and strains."

"Wow. That's a lot of ailments."

She read a little further. "The main ingredients were morphine and alcohol."

He grinned. "Well, that explains it. That recipe would make you feel better no matter what ails you."

They had a long drive through Maine to the motel they were staying at that night. Halfway there, Matthew gave Anne a dress with puffed sleeves.

When they stopped for a bathroom break, Jane showed him a picture of a dress from 1910 to explain what the hell puffed sleeves were.

He shook his head. "I'm with Marilla on this one. Those things look ridiculous. Thank God women's clothes have gotten more practical."

Jane laughed. "Not really. Do you remember the blue silk dress in that store window? *Wear this and find the man of your dreams?* That had puffed sleeves. Not this big, but they were definitely puffed."

He shook his head again. "I don't get why you'd want to wear something that serves no useful purpose."

"You mean like a cowboy hat?"

"Are you kidding? My Stetson keeps my head cool and shades my eyes. It's the definition of useful."

"Well, the point of art and fashion and all that isn't just to be useful. It's like the *Book of Kells*."

Her mind had made one of those leaps again, leaving him struggling to follow.

"The book of what?"

"It's this medieval illuminated manuscript. The calligraphy and illustrations are incredibly elaborate. Irish monks spent years on it, sometimes taking months to decorate a single letter."

"And your point?"

"They didn't need to do that. It wasn't *useful*. I mean, the text was the four Gospels of the Bible. They could have just written out the words. But they spent years, maybe decades, illuminating them with this gorgeous calligraphy. To the glory of God."

"I refuse to believe that puffed sleeves have anything to do with God."

Jane laughed. "No. But doing more than what's strictly necessary is part of what makes us human. We make flourishes. Gestures."

"If you say so." He turned the audiobook back on. "I just want to see what happens next."

What happened next was that Anne had to cut off her hair, after accidentally dying it green.

She also nearly drowned in the Lake of Shining Waters (at least now he knew what that was) and had to be rescued by Gilbert.

In the book, the lake was originally called Barry's Pond. But Anne, who had an imagination like Jane's, had a habit of renaming places and had christened it the Lake of Shining Waters instead.

"And it's a real lake? I mean, a real place in real life?"

Jane nodded. "Well, a pond, anyway. In a town called Cavendish, which is what Avonlea is based on."

"Is that scene the reason Horn-Rims picked it for his meeting? Because Gilbert rescues Anne there?"

"I don't know. Maybe?"

"I guess you could consider that romantic. Except that Anne snaps at Gilbert even after he rescues her."

"But she—"

"She always snaps at Gilbert. Or pretends he doesn't exist."

"That's not—"

"For a mistake he made five years before and totally apologized for. And she broke her slate over his head when it happened, so they should have called it even."

Watching her out of the corner of his eye, he could see Jane gathering herself up to deliver a stinging defense of her favorite book. Then she must have noticed the quirk at one corner of his mouth, because she relaxed and contented herself with a dignified glare.

"I'd be happy to turn the book off if you're so unimpressed with it." She'd called his bluff.

"You might as well leave the damn thing on now. I mean, we've made it this far."

By the time they pulled into the parking lot of the Owl Mountain Motor Lodge, Anne had won a scholarship to go to college, and she and Gilbert still hadn't made up.

He turned off the engine but not the power, waited for a break in the narration, and paused the audio. "How much more is there to go? Maybe we should stay here and listen to the end."

Jane grinned at him. "So you're buying dinner, huh?"

He couldn't stop himself from reaching out the way he used to, giving her braid a quick tug. "Yeah, you win. It's a good story. So should we listen to the end or what?"

She shook her head. "I'm starving, and there's forty-five minutes left. We can listen to the rest tomorrow."

"Fine, whatever. Don't encourage my newfound love of literature. See if I care."

She rolled her eyes at him, and he realized suddenly that after ten hours in the car listening to a hundred-year-old children's book, things between them were as close to normal as they'd been since before Sam's death.

Relief spread through him as he reached to unplug the phone, and she reached out at the same time.

Their hands touched.

How many times in his life had his hand brushed a woman's? Whether it happened accidentally or on purpose, that one hint of contact could tell you everything you needed to know about your chemistry with another person.

Touching Sam had felt secure and familiar, like touching a sibling. Touching the last woman he'd dated had felt anonymous, as though if he'd taken her hand in the dark, he wouldn't have been able to tell her apart from anyone else.

But he would know Jane's hand with his eyes closed in a roomful of strangers.

It wasn't just the electricity that made the fine hairs on his forearms stand up. It was the feel of her skin and her faint, unmistakable scent, like sunlight and cinnamon. It was the click that happened somewhere deep inside him, as though magnet and metal had come together.

His fingers closed over hers before he knew what he was doing. Their eyes met for one instant, but Jane's expression was startled and wary. She pulled her hand away and opened her door.

Chapter Sixteen

Jane had been half joking when she'd started the audiobook, figuring Caleb would put up with it for ten minutes before insisting on music. Then, after an hour had gone by, she'd assumed he was humoring her.

Until she realized he was actually caught up in the story.

Anne had always been special to her. The girl with the wild imagination, the girl who loved books, the girl who saw fairies in raindrops and thought amethysts were the souls of good violets. The orphan who didn't belong, who was odd and plain and not quite like her peers, but who still managed to find a family and form friendships and even fall in love.

The part of herself that loved Anne was the part she'd been sure she could never share with Caleb. The part that, even if she did share it, she was sure he wouldn't understand.

That was one of the things she'd told herself this past winter, when the thought of him halfway around the world had been like a knife in her heart. She'd reminded herself that they had nothing in common, that a relationship between them would be impossible—and not just because he'd never stick around long enough to actually have one.

She closed the car door and leaned back against it, waiting for Caleb to get out and open the trunk. Her hand still tingled where he'd touched her.

The air was colder here than it had been in Brooklyn, and she wrapped her arms around her waist for warmth. It was dark, too, the few lights of the motel not doing much against the pitch-blackness of a rural Maine night. In the woods surrounding the parking lot, she could hear the rustling of trees and the hooting of owls and other sounds she couldn't identify, and she remembered with a sinking feeling that she'd be hiking into that wilderness tomorrow. During the drive, listening to a favorite book and trying not to admire the muscles in Caleb's arms and the ease and competence of his driving—the same ease and competence he brought to any physical task—she'd managed to forget about tomorrow's leg of their journey.

Behind her, she heard the driver's side door slam. When she turned, the sight of Caleb's broad shoulders reminded her of the weight of him above her, pressing her down into the couch cushions on a snowy night.

She shivered. Caleb was more dangerous to her peace of mind than any mountaintop.

He went around to the trunk. He left his pack in there but pulled out a small duffel along with her suitcase. When she reached for it, he shook his head.

"I've got it," he said, and his willingness to carry a burden for her—even just her suitcase—made her feel suddenly weak in the knees.

And that, of course, was the problem. She couldn't let herself get used to this feeling or to having Caleb around. With her only sister gone, she was living with a new kind of loneliness, and she needed to be strong. She couldn't let herself sink as low as she had last Christmas, especially since Caleb wouldn't be around to help her again.

He'd be in Australia or Venezuela or Bali—or anywhere but where she was.

When they went into the motel office, she had a sudden vision of how this would go if they were in a romantic comedy. In a movie, there'd be only one room available, and they'd have to share.

But this wasn't a movie. It was real life in rural Maine, and there were plenty of vacancies.

They took their room keys and went back outside. Their rooms were next to each other on the ground floor, not far from where Caleb had parked. Caleb handed Jane her suitcase before swiping his key card into his lock.

"Dinner's not going to be that elegant," he said, pausing in the doorway. "The motel sells premade sandwiches, and there are vending machines at the end of the building. I'll dump my stuff and grab us something. Anything you won't eat, sandwich-wise?"

"The only thing I don't like is egg salad."

"Got it."

He started to go into his room, but she grabbed his arm. "Caleb."

He paused. "Yeah?"

"Could I borrow the car keys?"

"Sure, but what for? There's nothing in there except . . ." He stopped.

She felt like an idiot. "It's just . . . the weather app on my phone says it's going to get down into the forties tonight. I don't . . . I don't want to leave her out in the cold."

He looked at her for a second and then fished the keys out of his pocket.

"Here you go," he said. "I'll get us some food."

Her hand closed around the keys. "Thanks."

She opened the back door and lifted the urn out. It felt heavy in her arms—heavier than it had that morning, as though it had gotten bigger or she'd gotten weaker. She carried it into her room, looked around, and set the urn down on a cheap-looking bureau under the ugliest painting she'd ever seen in her life. It appeared to be a farmhouse at sunset done by a grade-school kid with a set of neon markers.

She looked at the urn, touching one of the white seagulls with a fingertip.

"I should just leave you here to spend eternity with the most hideous painting in the universe. It would serve you right for dying."

There was a knock on the door, and she went to let Caleb in.

He was holding a saran-wrapped sandwich in one hand—ham and cheese, it looked to be—and a Diet Coke in the other.

"Your dinner," he said with a smile. "Congrats on winning your bet." He glanced over her shoulder into the room, his gaze falling on the urn. "Do you want company? I could grab my sandwich and eat in here with you."

She shook her head. "No, that's okay. I'm just going to watch some TV and go to sleep."

"Good idea. We need to get an early start tomorrow."

"How early?"

"I'd like to be at the trailhead by eight. It's ten minutes from here, so we should leave around seven forty-five."

She sighed. "I can't believe you're making me do this."

He grinned at her. "You can't pin this on me. Your sister was the one who told you exactly where to scatter her ashes. I'm just the chauffeur."

She sighed again. "Good night, chauffeur. Thanks for dinner."

He handed her the sandwich and soda. "Good night, Jane."

Then he was gone, pulling the door closed behind him.

She ate in bed, watching an old episode of *Law and Order* and wishing she'd brought a book with her. She had e-books on her phone, but tonight she craved one of her battered old paperbacks, smelling a little musty, with lines in the corners where she'd dog-eared pages over the years.

She felt wide awake after eating, and the urge to go next door and see Caleb was overwhelming. But she could feel the fault line in her heart where he was concerned, and she knew the wrong kind of pressure there would crack her wide open.

Tomorrow she would be scattering Sam's remains from the top of a mountain. That was enough emotion to deal with right now.

It was only nine o'clock, but she had a big hike tomorrow and should get as much sleep as possible. She took a shower, not bothering with soap or shampoo once she discovered there wasn't much water pressure, and braided her damp hair afterward.

A hot shower—even one with lousy water pressure—could usually soothe her into sleepiness, but she knew as soon as her head hit the pillow that it wasn't going to work tonight.

She tossed and turned for an hour before giving up. She craved a cup of tea or hot chocolate, and she wondered if the vending alcove had an appliance that dispensed hot drinks.

A few minutes later she learned that the answer was no. She settled for iced tea even though it was sweetened and flavored with lemon, which she hated. When the bottle rumbled down from the innards of the machine, she grabbed it and started back toward her room.

She was still in the shadows near the vending area when she spotted a figure standing outside her door.

She froze and moved closer to the wall, not wanting to be seen. An instant later she realized it was Caleb, and relief flooded through her.

It must be his own door he was standing in front of, not hers. But as she waited for him to go inside, it occurred to her that his behavior was a little odd.

He was standing absolutely still with his hands and his forehead pressed against the door.

Was he okay? A part of her wanted to emerge from the shadows and go up to him, but what then? An awkward conversation in the middle of the night?

What the heck was he doing, anyway?

Eventually he pushed himself away from the door, but he still didn't go inside. Instead, he crossed the parking lot to their car and got in the driver's seat.

Where could he be going at this hour? They were in the middle of nowhere.

She waited, but the engine didn't start. After a minute she realized it wasn't going to and that, for some reason, Caleb just wanted to sit in the car for a while.

The reason was none of her business. She should go back to her room and try again to sleep.

Instead, she stood in the shadows by the vending machines and watched the car for five minutes.

Damn that man, anyway. What was he doing? She wouldn't be able to sleep until she was sure he was okay.

She crossed the parking lot and went up to the driver's side window. Caleb was frowning down at the steering wheel and didn't notice her. She rapped on the glass, and he jumped.

"Jesus Christ," he said, lowering the window. "You scared the shit out of me."

"I just wanted to see if you were okay," she said. "What are you—"

Then, suddenly, she heard a familiar voice.

"Marilla went to town the next day . . ."

"You're listening to *Anne of Green Gables*," she said, seeing Caleb's phone hooked up to the audio port.

He shrugged, looking embarrassed. "I downloaded it, but I don't have headphones with me. It sounded kind of tinny without the car's speakers, so I came out here."

She started to smile. "You're listening to the end of the book."

"I couldn't sleep," he said defensively. "And I wanted to know how it turned out." He paused. "Matthew dies," he said, almost accusingly.

She went around to the passenger side and got in beside him. "You can't be mad at me because a fictional character died."

Caleb shifted in his seat to face her. "Are you saying you didn't feel sad when you read that part?"

"No, I totally did. But Matthew lived a long and full life. And he's fictional."

Caleb didn't look convinced. "I didn't think this was the kind of book where someone would die. I mean, it's a kids' book. It sort of took me by surprise."

She reached out and un-paused the audio. "Let's listen to the rest."

And so they sat in the cold, dark car and listened to the last chapter together. After it was done, they sat for a minute in silence.

"So, did you like it?"

Caleb nodded. "Yeah. I'm glad Anne and Gilbert finally made up. They waited until the very end of the book, though."

"I know, but they have plenty of time together in the rest of the series. They fall in love and get married and have kids."

"It's a series? Damn. Are you going to make me listen to more books?"

Jane smiled. "No, the first one's the best." She paused. "But isn't it nice to know that Anne and Gilbert have a happy ending, out there in bookland?"

"Yeah, I guess it is." He unplugged his phone and slid it into his pocket. "It's pretty cold out here. We should probably—"

"Wait."

She put a hand on his shoulder, and a little tingle of electricity shot up her arm.

She pulled her hand back as he turned to look at her.

"What?"

"I want . . ." She swallowed. "I want you to tell me something."

He looked puzzled. "Sure."

"I want you to tell me why you always spend Christmas alone."

With the phone unplugged and the car's power off, it was dark in the front seat of the car. Maybe it would be easier for Caleb to tell her something personal in the dark, when they couldn't really see each other's faces.

When he didn't answer her right away, she felt a little encouraged. He could've just said no and left, after all. But he was still here.

"You know the worst thing that ever happened to me," she said after a moment. "Can't you tell me the worst thing that ever happened to you?"

Caleb shifted in his seat. "See, now, this is what happens when a woman sees you cry over a children's book. She thinks she can ask all kinds of personal questions."

She could tell by the tone of his voice that he wasn't going to walk away.

"Did you actually cry about Matthew? Seriously?"

"There might have been a few tears." He paused. "Okay. Well. My father killed himself when I was twelve years old."

It was like a punch in the gut. She'd expected to hear about a death, but she'd thought it would be cancer or a car accident.

Not this.

"Oh, Caleb." A horrible thought occurred to her. "He didn't do it at Christmas?"

Caleb gave a short laugh. "No, he was very careful not to do it at Christmas. Or on New Year's Day. In his suicide note, he explained that he didn't want me and my brother to associate 'the event' with any special date. So he waited until December 27." He paused. "But that only meant the entire fucking holiday season was associated with 'the event.'"

She didn't know what to say. But Caleb was still talking, and maybe all she had to do was listen.

"You might think, if he was so concerned, that he would have waited a month or two. Or three, even. March would have been perfect. No holidays in March, right? Except for Saint Patrick's Day, and who gives a shit about Saint Patrick's Day?"

Her insides were all twisted up. She tried to imagine one of her parents doing something like that and what it would have done to her.

Caleb shifted to face her. "And then, if he made it to March, he might have decided he could wait until summer. And then fall. And then winter again. And then it might have occurred to him that maybe he shouldn't fucking kill himself at all, because no matter when he did it, he'd be blowing a hole in our lives that could never be fixed."

There was a long silence, and the cold and the dark seemed to deepen. She wanted to warm Caleb up somehow, the way he'd warmed her up last December, but that would involve leaving the car for the motel, and she couldn't seem to move.

"So where do you go at Christmas?" she asked softly.

"Hiking. Different places, but always by myself . . . and always somewhere with ice and snow."

"Why?" Another terrible thought occurred to her. "You don't . . . you're not hoping to die, are you?"

He shook his head. "Just the opposite. Solo hiking in winter is dangerous. One mistake can cost your life." He paused. "It's a reminder that being alive isn't easy. It's a struggle. You have to work for it. And every time I do, I'm reminding myself that I don't want to die."

She remembered him last December, coming into her apartment and working, cleaning, cooking, taking on all the basic tasks of life she'd let go. Making sure she had food to eat and a hot drink and clean sheets to sleep on.

She thought about what he did for a living. And she remembered the story Sam had told, about the boy with the broken leg Caleb had carried for three miles.

He knew how to keep himself warm in the wilderness, but he could keep other people warm, too. If someone was in his care, he'd do whatever it took to keep them safe.

"Why did your father do it? Did he say in the note?"

"No. He just said he was sorry and that he hoped we could forgive him."

"Why do you think he did it?"

"A lot of reasons. My mother had left a year before, and he never got over it. And the ranch was struggling. It had been in our family for five generations, and he was afraid he'd be the one to lose it."

All the years she'd known him, and he'd never told her any of this. "Your mother left? Where is she now?"

"Who knows. Tijuana, maybe? She calls once in a while. She's a singer, likes to travel. My father met her at some honky-tonk in Colorado Springs back in the day and swept her off her feet." It was hard to tell in the darkness, but she thought he smiled. "Women love a cowboy. At first, anyway."

His father dead by suicide, and his mother off on the road somewhere. Her heart ached at the thought of the eleven-year-old boy whose mother had abandoned him and the twelve-year-old boy whose father had killed himself.

"Your mother didn't come back after your father died?"

"No. Not even for the funeral."

God, that was brutal. "Was that when your aunt moved to the ranch?"

"Yeah. She was a CPA in Denver, but after Dad died, she moved out to the ranch and never looked back. She was like a mom to Hunter and me, and a business genius to boot. She got that place humming like a buzz saw. It's still a working ranch, but she turned part of it into a dude ranch. People come from all over to stay there."

Caleb often spoke about his aunt Rosemary and his brother Hunter. But he usually talked about what they were doing now, seldom delving into the past. The few stories she'd heard about Caleb's childhood had been about animals, not people. The horses he'd trained and the dog he'd grown up with who was part wolf, part husky, and tried to go with him to school every September. She and Sam had learned that you couldn't make Caleb answer any question he didn't want to.

He'd never said a word about any of this.

Caleb reached out and tugged on her braid. "I bet you're wishing you hadn't asked me why I spend Christmas alone."

She tried to ignore the little tingles at the back of her neck. "I'm not wishing that at all. Why would you think so?"

He shrugged. "I don't know. It's a depressing story."

"But it's your story. I'm glad you told me." A wave of guilt went through her. "After Sam died, I didn't think about you. I only thought about my own grief. But you loved Sam as much as I did. And you've lost more people you love than I have."

"It's not a contest," he said gently.

"I know. But when you came to see me in December, you took care of me. I wish I'd tried to take care of you, too."

He shook his head. "Don't you know I'd rather take care of you than the other way around?"

There was another silence, but this one felt different somehow. She was trying to figure out how when Caleb spoke again.

"Jane?"

"Yes?"

"Do you ever think about that night?"

Chapter Seventeen

The cold disappeared, driven away by adrenaline and her pounding heart. Blood rushed to every corner of her body.

"No," she said.

He moved in the darkness, and she was aware of his size, his power. In an instant, everything had changed. They'd been talking about the past, thinking about the past, but now it was as if the past had never been and the future didn't matter.

There was only the present.

"Liar."

"I'm not—"

"You're thinking about it right now."

She pressed herself back against the car door. She'd given in to this feeling last December because she'd felt so lost, and because she wanted him so much, and because she'd convinced herself that since the world was such a shithole she might as well have one good thing, one moment of bliss in all the emptiness and grief. She'd known it wouldn't last, but in December it hadn't mattered.

Now it did.

"Well, of course I'm thinking about it *now*," she said. "You just brought it up."

"I bet you think about it all the time. I bet you think about me every night."

God, did she? There had to be some nights she didn't think about Caleb in those vulnerable moments right before sleep came.

"I do not."

"Yeah, you do. You know how I know?"

"I—"

"Because I think about you every night, too."

Her heart stopped.

"I think about the snow falling outside and your Harry Potter pajamas and how goddamn beautiful you looked. I think about your nails on my back and your legs around my waist. I think about sinking inside you and wanting to stay there forever. I think about the look on your face when you came."

She closed her eyes. "Caleb—"

"It's okay."

She opened her eyes again, wondering how she could have ever thought it was cold in here. Her body was like a furnace.

Caleb looked at her for a moment, and she wished she could see his face.

Then he reached behind him to open the door, and a draft of cold air came in to cool the fever in her cheeks.

"Don't worry," he said. "I know it's not going to happen again. I just wanted you to know that I think about it." He paused. "Good night, Jane."

He got out of the car and slammed the door behind him, and she watched him cross the parking lot and go into his room.

"Good night, Caleb," she whispered.

◆ ◆ ◆

When morning came, a steady rain was falling.

Jane sat up in bed and looked out at the grayness. It was just after dawn, and the slate-colored sky looked full of more rain to come. Her heart sank into her toes at the thought of hiking up a mountain in that. Would it even be safe? Maybe Caleb would say they had to wait.

As though thinking of him had been a signal, there was a knock at her door.

A sudden flush spread from her neck to her face. Last night when she'd gone back to her room, she'd been unable to sleep. Her restlessness had eased only when she thought about Caleb, and thinking had led to . . .

Would he be able to tell somehow?

The knock came again, and she jumped out of bed. Of course Caleb wouldn't be able to tell. She was being ridiculous.

And anyway, he'd said he thought about her, too. Wasn't it likely that his thoughts led the same place hers had, at least once in a while?

Okay, wrong thing to focus on if she wanted the heat in her cheeks to subside.

She took a deep breath and opened the door.

Caleb was wearing some very professional-looking rain gear—jacket and pants—and equally professional-looking hiking boots.

He'd told her to buy a pair of boots or trail running shoes and break them in before their trip, but she'd decided that was too much trouble. She'd brought her sneakers instead.

She wondered what Caleb would say when he found out.

"You're not dressed yet," Caleb said, frowning at her.

He sounded critical, but that was better than *Hey, Jane, I can totally tell you were fantasizing about me last night.*

"I must have slept through my alarm." She hesitated. "So, I guess we're going ahead with the trip?"

"You mean because of the rain? We can wait a day if you want, but you might miss Horn-Rims at the bridge on May 1."

"No! We don't have to wait. It's just, uh, really wet." She hesitated again. "We could . . . well, skip the hike completely. I don't have to go now. It's not like there's a deadline or anything. I meant to go this summer, or even next year. We don't have to—"

But Caleb was already shaking his head. "You need to do this, Jane." Man, he could be bossy sometimes.

This time, though, she had a feeling he might be right.

"Fine. Give me five minutes?"

"Sure." He reached into a pocket and pulled out an impossibly tiny packet of material, shaking it out into a rain jacket and rain pants like the ones he wore. "I got these for you in the city in case of bad weather."

They looked to be her size. "Wow. Thank you."

"Wear warm layers. I'll be in the car," he said, and then he was gone.

Long underwear, flannel shirt, wool sweater, down jacket. Too much for the beginning of the hike, maybe—the temperature was in the sixties, mild in spite of the rain—but she was betting she'd be glad for the warmth when they got to the top of the mountain. And she could always carry what she didn't want to wear.

She put on the rain jacket and used the down jacket to cover Sam's urn, keeping it dry for the dash across the parking lot. She put it in the back seat like she had yesterday, buckling it in and then taking her seat next to Caleb.

"All set?" he asked.

She nodded. "All set."

It was quiet in the car without the audiobook in the background. The rain drummed against the roof, and when they pulled out of the parking lot and onto the road, the wipers couldn't go fast enough to keep up.

"So, it's definitely safe to hike in the rain, then?" she ventured after a few minutes.

"You need to be careful with your footing, especially if you're walking on mud or slick rocks, and you need to watch out for swollen creeks. But we should be fine, especially if you've got good"—he glanced at her feet—"shoes."

Oops.

"Well, they are good sneakers," she said defensively.

"They're not waterproof."

"No."

"They won't give you any ankle support."

"Well . . . no."

He sighed. "But it's just a day hike, so you should be all right. You might get blisters, though."

"Blisters? I don't want blisters."

"You should have brought decent shoes, then. But I'll do my best to take care of your feet."

They drove another few minutes in silence. "You know, I just thought of something."

He glanced at her. "Yeah?"

"I could sort of deputize you to go up the mountain for me. I'll stay down here in the car, and you can bring Sam's ashes up to the summit."

"Nice try."

"Is that a no?"

"Yes."

"Yes that's a no, or—"

"We're here."

He stopped the car in a deserted lot. A few yards away, she could see the beginning of a trail into the woods.

She couldn't see very far along it, but she assumed the trail led up the mountain looming in front of them, obscured by the rain, its top shrouded in mist like something out of *The Lord of the Rings*.

That thought made her feel a little more cheerful. If she could imagine this was a scene in a book, maybe she'd get through it better.

But any vision of this hike as a storybook adventure was dimmed when she opened the back door and picked up Sam's ashes. Whatever else this journey might be, it was the last one she'd ever take with her sister.

Caleb had brought a small pack for the urn, which was a relief. She hadn't even thought about the mechanics of carrying it, and in the moments between getting it out of the car and Caleb pulling the pack out of the trunk, she'd had a vision of herself holding it in her arms like a baby, all the way up the mountain.

The pack was the perfect size for the urn and her down jacket. She slung it over her shoulders, feeling the weight settle against her shoulder blades.

The rain was coming down as steadily as ever. In spite of the hood she'd pulled tight under her chin, droplets leaked under the edges and tickled her neck. She leaned against the car, head down, feeling wet and forlorn.

Suddenly Caleb was there, tilting her chin up with one hand.

"How you doing?" he asked, and the hint of amusement in his voice was more annoying than usual.

"I'm fine," she said.

His looming presence protected her from the rain, and she was able to glare up at him. He looked warm and dry and competent in his gear, unlike her, and even though the pack he carried was five times heavier than hers, he made it seem like nothing at all.

"Aren't you carrying a lot of stuff for a day hike?"

"We're going to the summit, the weather is shitty, and you're not an experienced hiker. Put all that together, and it's a plan-for-all-contingencies kind of trip. I'm hoping we won't need a third of what I'm bringing."

"Oh."

He smiled down at her. "Ready to go?"

"You bet."

He handed her two aluminum poles with wrist straps and soft grips for her hands.

"What are these?"

"Trekking poles," he said. "They'll help with your balance and your footing, and they'll absorb some of the shock as you're walking, which is good for your knees and ankles."

She slipped her hands through the straps. "Thanks."

"I'll lead the way," he said. "That way I'll be able to test out the terrain first, make sure it's stable. I won't be able to hear you very well, so give a shout if you need anything, okay? Or you could poke me in the back with one of your poles," he added with a grin.

He seemed remarkably cheerful in spite of the rain, and it occurred to her for the first time that out here, he was in his element. All the time they'd spent together in New York, he'd been in hers.

"Got it," she said.

"Okay, then. Here we go."

Her feet were soaked after only twenty minutes.

It was her own fault. They were crossing a shallow stream, the rushing water less than an inch deep where they forded it, but when she was distracted by a little frog she saw hopping from stone to stone, she'd stepped off the fording area and into water deep enough to cover her ankles.

Caleb hadn't seen, thank God. Feeling like a moron—a wet, uncomfortable moron—she clambered out of the stream and back onto the trail in time for Caleb to turn his head and check on her.

"Doing okay?" he asked.

"Absolutely," she said.

He set an easy pace—probably agonizingly slow to him—but it was still hard to keep up, and her wet feet didn't help. There was only one positive development as the trek went on. As they hiked deeper into the woods, the trees above them provided some protection from the rain, which went from a steady downpour beating on her head and shoulders to a slow, depressing drizzle.

But that small advantage was outweighed by the fact that the trail became steeper the farther they went. Her feet were already wet and aching, and now she felt the climb in her thighs and calves, too. Her muscles weren't used to this type of exercise, and they protested it loudly.

She became increasingly aware of the pack on her back, the weight of her sister's ashes growing heavier and heavier and the straps chafing her shoulders.

When they'd first started out, the pouring rain had encouraged her to keep her head down and her eyes on the ground. But as the trees overhead grew thicker, she could lift her head occasionally to watch Caleb walking ahead of her.

His stride never faltered, and he carried himself like the pack on his back weighed nothing at all. He was strong and tireless and competent, and as she watched him, she felt weak and tired and inept.

Finally, after what felt like an eternity, she poked him in the shoulder with the tip of a trekking pole.

"Hey!" she called out.

He turned instantly. "Hey yourself," he said with a grin. "How's it going back there?"

"I need a break. It feels like we've been going for hours."

"Well, forty-five minutes, anyway."

Her heart sank. Caleb had told her it would take three hours to reach the top of the mountain.

"That's it?"

He laughed, and even though there was no malice in it, at this particular moment it only added insult to injury.

"Stop laughing at me."

He came closer. "I'm not," he said, pulling a red bandanna from a pocket and using it to dry the raindrops from her face. "I'm laughing with you."

"Well, I'm not laughing," she grumbled. "Aren't we ever going to take a break?"

"Can you hang on a few more minutes? There's a lean-to up ahead where we can get off our feet and out of the rain."

That sounded like heaven.

"Okay. But it better only be a few minutes."

It was. They went forward a few hundred paces and around a bend, and then Caleb stepped off the trail and into a shelter made of logs. It had three walls and a roof and a floor of dead leaves, but best of all, there was a long, low bench at the back.

In her whole life, she'd never enjoyed the simple act of sitting down quite this much.

"It's beautiful, isn't it?" Caleb said after a minute.

With all her muscles mad at her, Caleb's pleasure felt like a personal affront. She turned to glare at him. He'd taken his pack and his jacket off and was leaning back, his thumbs hooked in his belt loops, his legs extended and one booted foot hooked over the other.

"What's beautiful? The rain?"

"Nature."

She wiggled her wet toes inside her sneakers.

"Nature can go fuck herself," she said, and Caleb threw back his head and laughed.

"I hardly ever hear you swear."

"I like to save it for worthy occasions."

He was looking out at the scene in front of them, and Jane followed the direction of his gaze.

Across the trail from where they were, a deep, tree-filled ravine dipped low and then rose up to a ridge, pale green and dark green and every shade in between. Sometime in the last hour the rain had let up a little, and she could see the far edge of the ridge clearly.

Beneath the trees around them, feathery clusters of soft ferns gave way, here and there, to bunches of wildflowers.

"It *is* beautiful," she said, and Caleb turned to smile at her.

"You sound surprised."

"I guess I was more focused on my feet."

She leaned forward, her eyes drawn to glimpses of white and purple and yellow and pink peeping out from beneath the trees and ferns.

"What are those?" she asked.

"The flowers?"

She nodded.

He pointed toward a little splash of white only a few yards away. "Lily of the valley." Then he pointed across the trail, where a river of luscious purple swept down from an enormous maple. "Violets," he said.

She thought of the book they'd listened to yesterday. "Like Anne's Violet Vale," she murmured.

He smiled. "Exactly." He looked right and left, as though searching for something, and when he found it he gave a grunt of satisfaction. "Something else from the book," he said, pointing to a little cluster of delicate pink blossoms.

"What are they?"

"Trailing arbutus." He paused. "Otherwise known as mayflowers."

She looked at them in delight. "Of course! Gilbert offered a bunch to Anne, but she rejected them with scorn."

He laughed. "Man, that girl was stubborn." He tilted his head to the side, thinking. "Remember what she said? She thought mayflowers were the souls of the flowers that died last summer, and this was their heaven."

She stared at him. "You remember that?"

"Sure. Don't you?"

"Well, yes. But I've read that book a hundred times. I practically know it by heart."

"I'm surprised you don't appreciate nature more, then. Anne loved nature."

"She did?"

He raised an eyebrow. "Yeah. Don't tell me you missed that."

She thought about it. "Not exactly. I mean, of course I remember the descriptions of nature, but I guess I wasn't as interested in those parts of the book. I noticed other things more."

"That was the thing I liked best about Anne." He paused. "The author loved nature, too, you know."

It was her turn to raise an eyebrow. "How in the world do you know that?"

He grinned. "I looked her up last night."

"Seriously?"

"Sure. There wasn't anything good on TV." He reached into an outer pocket on his pack and pulled out the waterproof bag that held his phone.

"Don't tell me you can get a signal out here," she said skeptically.

"I don't need one. I took screenshots of the quotes I liked."

"Quotes?"

"From L. M. Montgomery. Her letters and journals and things like that." He clicked through to something and handed her the phone. "Here."

She squinted down at the screen and read out loud. "Once and again, I stray down and listen to the duet of the brook and wind, and watch the sunbeams creeping through the dark boughs, the gossamers glimmering here and there, and the ferns growing up in the shadowy nooks."

He reached out with a fingertip and swiped right, bringing up a new screen.

She read aloud again. "It has always seemed to me that, amid all the commonplaces of life, I was very near to a kingdom of ideal beauty. Between it and me hung only a thin veil. I could never quite draw it aside, but sometimes a wind fluttered it and I caught a glimpse of the enchanting world beyond—only a glimpse, but those glimpses have always made life worthwhile."

She sat silent for a minute, goose bumps prickling her skin.

"I can't believe you actually looked up L. M. Montgomery," she said after a while.

He took his phone back. "Why not? Like I said, she loved nature. We're kindred spirits," he added, using one of Anne Shirley's favorite phrases.

He wrapped the phone up and returned it to his pack. "Besides, I make it a point to collect quotes about the natural world. It gives me something to tell people on trips. The best I can come up with on my own is 'Wow, pretty.' So it helps to have other people's words."

He pulled something else out of a different pocket—a red pouch marked First Aid. "Let's take a look at your feet."

"My feet?"

"I want to make sure they're okay."

"They're definitely not okay."

"Then let's do something about that." He held out his hands. "Give them here."

She turned to face him, swinging her feet up into his lap.

He unlaced her sneakers and pulled them off with a frown. "These are soaked through."

"Yep."

"Your socks, too."

"I know."

He reached into the pocket he'd taken the first aid kit from and pulled out a pair of clean, dry socks. "These will help."

She took them gratefully. "I take back everything I ever said about you. You're a god among men."

He pulled off her wet socks and used his red bandanna to dry her feet thoroughly.

"A couple of hot spots here," he said, examining her heels and arches.

"Hot spots?"

She was trying to be as clinical about this process as Caleb was, but the touch of his big hands on her bare skin felt anything but clinical.

"Points of friction that can turn into blisters," he explained, taking ointment and bandages out of the first aid kit and applying them to her feet—two on her heels and one on a big toe. "There," he said, taking the dry socks from her and sliding them on. Then he pulled out two plastic sandwich bags, put them over her socks, and put the sneakers back on over the bags. "That'll help keep you a little drier."

She put her feet back on the ground, marveling at the difference dry skin could make to a person's comfort.

"Got any other miracles in that pack of yours?"

He reached inside the main compartment. "It's not a miracle, but—" He pulled out a thermos, and when he opened it a curl of steam rose into the air. The aroma was deliciously familiar.

"Coffee!"

"With cream and lots of sugar, just the way you like it."

He poured out a cupful into the plastic lid and handed it to her.

The heat felt wonderful against her cold hands, and the coffee was the most delicious she'd ever tasted.

"I love you," she said without thinking. When she saw Caleb's expression, she cleared her throat. "I mean, I love this coffee."

"Uh-huh." He pulled a protein bar out of the pack and handed it to her. "How about now?"

She hadn't realized how ravenous she was until this moment. "Okay, I really do love you."

They were just joking around, but she was surprised at how easily the words came and how natural it felt to say them to him.

She waited, but Caleb didn't say anything else. After a moment she tore open her protein bar and bit into it.

Yes, they were just joking—but it wouldn't actually kill him to say it back to her. Even a flippant *I love you* shouldn't be left hanging.

She wouldn't say anything else, she decided. She'd let him be the next one to speak. *I love you, too.* Was that so hard? He could say it while tugging her braid or punching her on the shoulder.

After a few minutes, Caleb slung his pack over his shoulders and rose to his feet.

"All set?" he asked. "We've still got a long way to go."

Chapter Eighteen

Her feet stayed dry all the way to the top of the mountain.

She found herself paying attention to what was around her on the second half of the hike, instead of wallowing in the internal world of her own discomfort. She felt a thrill every time she spotted a cluster of white or yellow or purple or pink, and she put out a hand to feel the softness of fern fronds.

The trees, too, were beautiful. They seemed ancient and wise, weathered and patient, and the scent of moss and pine sap was sharp and invigorating.

It seemed to wake her up somehow—and to give her a second wind of strength and endurance that carried her to the summit. Or maybe it was Sam's spirit, encouraging her and cajoling her and reminding her of the story she'd told so long about this very place.

It was my first solo hike, and when I got to the top . . . well, you'll see when you go. It's the reason I decided to become a trek guide. There might be more famous mountains and spectacular views out there, but Owl Mountain is my mountain.

She'd only ever understood this part of Sam from a distance. Intellectually rather than emotionally. But now . . .

She was glad Caleb had made her do this.

The quotes he'd showed her echoed in her mind. It was amazing that even after reading about Anne Shirley a hundred times, there were still facets of the character she hadn't appreciated. If that could be true of a fictional character, how much more true was it about real human beings? What else hadn't she understood about her own sister?

Or Caleb?

She thought about what he'd told her last night and what they were doing now. His mother had walked out and his father had killed himself, and this was what Caleb had decided to do with his life.

This was his way of choosing light over darkness. He devoted himself to the natural world, and he helped others appreciate it, too.

The rain stopped when they were close to the summit, but Caleb didn't look happy about it.

"There's fog rolling in," he said. "We won't have much of a view."

He was right. When they finally reached the top, the mist was so thick it felt like they were walled in on the rocky plateau.

She looked around. For all she could see, they might not have been on a mountaintop at all. There was just the tableland where they stood, dotted with boulders and bushes and stunted trees, and the prison of fog around them. The wind was strong and bitter cold, which somehow made the rocks and straggling spruce trees seem lonelier and more desolate.

"I'm sorry," Caleb said. "I was hoping you'd get something spectacular as a reward for all your hard work."

He set his pack down beside a large boulder, but she kept hers on. He headed for the leeward side of the plateau, and she followed.

They stood there for a while, just looking out at the white wall of cloud, until finally Caleb turned to her.

"This is the best place," he said. "You'll want the wind at your back."

She wasn't sure what he was talking about.

"The best place for what?"

He nodded toward her pack. "The best place to scatter Sam's ashes."

The shock that went through her was like stepping into icy water.

"Oh no," she said, the words jerked out of her.

Caleb frowned. "I guess we can walk around a little, but—"

"No. No. This place is fine. It's just . . ." She slid her hands into her pockets and clenched them into fists. "I'm not ready. Not yet."

He looked at her for a moment and then nodded.

"Okay." He glanced at his watch. "We only have an hour, though. We need to make it down to the car before it gets dark."

"I understand." She looked out at the fog. "I just need some time."

"Do you want something to eat? Something to drink?"

She shook her head. "No, I'm fine."

He put a hand on her shoulder. "Do you want company? Or do you want to be alone?"

She liked that he gave her that choice. She realized, suddenly, that Caleb would always give someone that choice. He understood the need for solitude.

"I think I want to be alone. With . . ." She hesitated. "With Sam."

Would he think that was strange? Morbid?

"Okay," he said. "If you need me, I won't be far."

She watched him walk away, thinking, *You'll be far when you go back to Australia.*

It was a lonely thought, and she almost called out for him to come back. But then she set her pack on the ground, traded her rain jacket for her down jacket, and sat down on a flat rock with her sister's ashes in her lap.

She wondered what Sam would say if she were here.

Just scatter the damn things already.

She squeezed her eyes shut, feeling the bitter wind on her face.

I can't. I can't let you go.

What else are you going to do? Stay up here forever?

Maybe.

Don't be ridiculous, little sis. Scatter my ashes and get on with your life.

She put the urn back in the pack and zipped it up.

I hate you for leaving me.

I know.

I miss you.

I know.

And all around her the wind blew, and the fog closed in, and the weight on her lap grew heavier and heavier until she thought it would pull her down through the mountain into the depths of the earth.

◆ ◆ ◆

Caleb gave her forty-five minutes before going back to the edge of the plateau.

She looked small and lonely as he drew closer, sitting cross-legged with her arms wrapped around the pack in her lap.

He put a hand on her shoulder and squeezed gently.

"It's time."

She looked up, and he saw the streaks of tears on her face.

"No."

He frowned. "What do you mean, no?"

She wiped her eyes with the back of her hand. "Sam asked me to go hiking with her all the time, and I always said no. I know it's too late now, but I feel like I'm learning something about her up here. Something I never understood before." She gestured around her. "I can't let her go yet. I can't." She paused. "I want to stay here tonight."

He stared at her. "Are you kidding? It'll be below freezing up here. We have to start hiking down right now."

She shook her head, her expression stubborn, and he'd never seen her look more like Samantha.

"Didn't you bring a tent? You must have something in that huge pack besides coffee and Band-Aids."

He squatted down beside her. "I brought camping equipment because we were going on a long hike in bad weather, but it's only for emergencies."

Jane's face was pinched with cold, but her expression was resolute. "Well, consider this an emergency. Because I'm not leaving."

His need to get her down the mountain and into a warm motel room grew more urgent.

"Jane—"

"I'm not leaving."

He knew that look. He'd seen it on Sam's face often enough.

He glared at her. "You're going to have to scatter her ashes eventually, you know. Unless you're planning to stay here forever?"

Her eyes lowered. "I don't want to stay here forever," she said softly. "I just want to stay here tonight."

He sighed in frustration, his breath misting in the cold.

And it was only going to get colder.

He could sit here and argue with her, he could try to drag her down the mountain by force, or he could go back to his pack and start making some kind of camp.

He surged to his feet. "I can't believe how pissed I am at you right now."

She looked up at him again, her eyes grateful. "Thank you, Caleb."

"Don't thank me. I'm close to throwing you off this damn mountain."

She smiled. "Thank you," she said again.

He didn't say anything else. He just trudged back the way he'd come, leaving Jane and Samantha to wrestle with eternity.

◆　◆　◆

He found a relatively sheltered spot to pitch the tent. By the time Jane came back, he had the WhisperLite stove going behind its windshield.

They had plenty of water, so he poured two cups into his battered cooking pot and waited for it to boil.

Jane watched him for a moment before she spoke. "What's for dinner?"

She sounded conciliatory, like she was hoping all was forgiven.

He glowered at her. "If you'd bothered to listen to me, it could have been pizza or Chinese food or a Big Mac. As it is, we're stuck with whatever freeze-dried crap I threw in the pack yesterday. I don't even know what I brought." He tossed the sack with the food over to her. "You pick."

He was sitting on one of their sleeping bags, still rolled up, and she sat down on the other one as she looked through the sack.

"Oatmeal. Applesauce. Ramen noodles. This is kind of uninspiring."

"So help me, if you complain about the menu choices—"

She smiled. "This one looks like some kind of pasta. That might be okay. Wait, no . . . this is the one." She pulled out a bag. "Chili!"

He held out a hand. "Toss it over."

The chili reconstituted in the boiling water and bubbled slowly over the blue flames. He gave it ten minutes and served it in two tin cups.

He handed Jane a spoon. "Bon appétit."

It tasted delicious, the way food on the trail always did. Between hunger and exercise and the cold mountain air, anything would have seemed like a feast. But this was a high-end brand of freeze-dried food for backpackers, with enough spice to give it a kick and enough beans and protein to make it filling.

They both had a second helping.

"I can't believe how good that was," Jane said. She'd finished a few minutes ago, but her hands were wrapped around the still-warm tin cup.

"Yeah. Food always tastes better outside."

He started to clean up.

"Can I help?" she asked.

He shook his head. "Just keep me company. Tell me something about Sam I don't know. Something from your childhood."

"Like what?"

"Tell me about a time you were jealous of her."

She was quiet for a moment. "Why would you want to hear about that?"

"Because it's part of the way you feel about her. Part of growing up with her."

"I suppose that's true." She thought for a while. "Well. On my thirteenth birthday, we were supposed to have a party. Just the family, because we'd only moved from New York to LA that month. But the party never happened, because Sam had won this big track competition and the state finals were that day. So we went to that, and it was three hours away. We stopped for dinner on the way home instead of having a party at our house. My parents called it a joint celebration, because Sam had won a gold medal and I was turning thirteen."

"Man." The stove and cups and utensils were packed away, and afternoon was turning to evening. "That must have pissed you off but good."

Jane wrapped her arms around her waist. "It sounds so petty to talk about it now."

"No, it doesn't. It sounds like you grew up with a really annoying older sister."

"She wasn't annoying. Not exactly."

"She won things all the time, didn't she?"

"Yes."

"My older brother was the junior rodeo champion of Colorado three years in a row. He annoyed the hell out of me."

She smiled in spite of herself. "Okay, maybe you're right."

It was too cold to sit still much longer. He got to his feet and held out a hand to help Jane up.

"Let's go for a walk," he said, and they started across the plateau. "Tell me the nicest thing Sam ever did for you."

Jane didn't have to think about that one. "She took me to London to meet J. K. Rowling."

He stared at her. "She did? I never knew that."

"It was her junior year in college, before you guys met. She had to make a charity contribution to get into the event, and she bought the plane tickets and paid for a hotel room." She paused. "It wasn't just the money, though. She was supposed to be in this big swim meet the day we left. She was favored to win the hundred-meter butterfly."

They walked in silence for another minute or two, and then suddenly Jane stopped.

"It's getting darker. I wasn't sure before, but now I am. It's definitely getting darker."

"Yeah," he said. "That's a thing that happens."

She looked up at him, and her face was frightened. "It's too late to go back down now. We're stuck here."

He took her hand and started walking again. "It was too late a while ago, darlin'. But don't worry. I've got you."

He wasn't sure if his words reassured her or not. But as they made a loop around the mountaintop that led them back to their camp, they echoed in his mind.

I've got you.

It was a phrase he'd used often enough on treks, helping people over obstacles or up steep inclines or across swift-moving rivers. But this felt different somehow.

Bigger. More important.

Back at the camp, he unrolled their sleeping bags and laid them out in the tent. It was designed for three people, so there was plenty of room.

He came back outside and saw Jane standing with her back to him, looking out over the darkening plateau. Before long they wouldn't be able to see anything at all.

He came up beside her and the two of them waited, watching, while gray turned to black. Except for the faint glow from his flashlight inside the tent, the darkness was complete.

He took her hand. "We may as well go to sleep," he said. "That'll be the best way to stay warm until morning."

He sensed rather than saw the shake of her head. "I'm going to stay out here."

His anger from earlier in the day returned. "No, you're not. The wind's picking up, and the temperature's dropping. Come on, Jane. Get inside the tent."

"I'm going to stay out here," she said again.

He could feel his temper rising. "What the hell for? Some kind of vigil? Some kind of penance, like last December?"

"No!"

"Then what, damn it? What are you going to do out here?"

The light from the tent was very faint, but his eyes had adjusted enough that he could see the outline of her body, her face.

"I don't know."

"Jane—"

She took a step back. "Just leave me alone, okay? I'll be all right. Just let me be."

"If you go wandering around in the dark—"

"I won't. And anyway, I have that little flashlight you gave me."

"It's still not safe to walk a summit at night. I swear to God, Jane, if you kill yourself up here—"

"You think I'd let that happen, after what your father did to you? After we both lost Sam?"

He swallowed. "I'm not saying you'd do it on purpose. But if you get too close to the edge—"

"I won't. You have to trust me. Please, Caleb. I won't wander off, and I won't get hurt."

A kind of rage rose in his heart. Jane wouldn't come in where it was warm, and there was nothing he could do about it.

"I could make you," he said. "I could drag you in that tent and stuff you inside your sleeping bag."

"I know you could. But you won't."

They stood there for a moment, staring at each other in the dark. The tension between them crackled like static.

Finally he sighed. "In my entire life, I've never met a woman as stubborn as you—and that includes your sister." He took off his down jacket and handed it to her. "At least take this."

"I'm already wearing a jacket."

"So wear two, damn it."

She took it from him meekly. "All right."

He turned his back on her and went inside the tent. He undressed down to his long underwear and slid inside his sleeping bag, his body heat beginning to warm the space almost immediately.

He left the flashlight on. Jane had one with her, but he wanted her to be able to find the tent immediately whenever she was ready to come in.

Then he rolled over on his side, away from the light and toward the wall of the tent, and tried to go to sleep.

Chapter Nineteen

He must have succeeded, because when he opened his eyes again, he knew time had passed.

He lifted his wrist to check his watch. It was just after midnight.

Turning his head, he saw that Jane wasn't beside him. He slid out of his sleeping bag, clenched his teeth against the cold, and unzipped the tent flap.

There were a million stars in the sky.

Sometime in the night, the fog had lifted. The air was clear and bitter, and by the light of the stars he could see Jane standing a few yards away.

She'd turned her head at the sound of the tent zipper. She was wearing his jacket, and it was big enough that she'd been able to put it over her pack, too, which made her look like an oddly shaped rock formation.

She stood so still that she might have been a statue, except for the gleam of starlight in her eyes.

"It's so cold," she said after a moment.

His boots were just outside the tent. He put them on and went to stand beside Jane, shivering in his long underwear.

"You know, you're right," he said through chattering teeth. "It is a little chilly."

"Do you want your jacket back?"

"No, I'm good. I'll be going back inside the tent soon, and you'll be coming with me."

She didn't say anything to that right away. Then: "I thought if I stayed out here, I'd have an epiphany or something. I thought . . . maybe . . . an answer would come."

She tilted her head up, looking at the stars, and he followed the direction of her gaze. The Milky Way was clearly visible, and he traced the constellations along its path: Orion, Perseus, Cassiopeia.

"An answer to what?" he asked after a moment. "What's the question?"

"Why Sam died. Where she is now."

He looked at the misshapen lump on her back, where she'd been carrying Sam's ashes for so long.

"She's not in there."

"I know that," Jane said. Then her eyes closed. "God, I'm so cold."

"Come in where it's warm."

"I don't have my answers yet."

He took her by the hand. "Maybe there aren't any answers. Not the kind you're looking for, anyway."

She opened her eyes and looked up at the sky. "That sounds so hopeless."

He wished he could do what she did so easily—put his thoughts and feelings into words. But at least he could try.

He squeezed her hand. "Look at the stars."

"I have been. They make me feel lonely."

"All those lights in the darkness? How can that make you feel lonely?"

"Because they don't have anything to say to me. If there aren't any answers, what is there?"

His throat tightened. "People who love you."

The wind was as cold as a knife, and maybe that was why she trembled. "Caleb—"

He stepped in close and kissed her.

The cold was so numbing that there shouldn't have been any sensation. But the moment his lips touched hers, electricity sizzled through his body. He wrapped his arms around her, finding her shoulders under the layers of down.

She was shaking. He didn't know if it was from the cold or from the same thing he was feeling. Then she leaned into him, and heat danced through his body.

He could die right here on this mountain, and a kiss from Jane would bring him back to life.

He didn't say anything after he broke the kiss. He just took her by the hand and led her back to the tent, and this time she came with him.

He kicked off his shoes before going inside, and she did the same. Then he helped her out of her jacket and lifted the pack from her shoulders.

"Strip down to your skin," he said, grabbing their two sleeping bags to zip them together.

The double-wide sleeping bag was ready by the time Jane had shivered out of her clothes, and she slid inside. After he shed his long underwear, he slid in beside her.

He pulled her into his arms. Her body was like an icicle, but it warmed quickly against his, and he held her tight as her muscles went from rigid to relaxed.

"You feel so good," she murmured against his chest, and he remembered the last time she'd said those words to him.

His body hardened. After last December, he would have sworn he'd never want anything like he'd wanted Jane that night. But this felt deeper and wilder. Talking to Jane about his parents last night, hiking with her today, had widened the crack in his heart that Jane had first put there so long ago. For years she'd been pushing against it and pushing against it until now, suddenly, it split apart.

It was like a dam breaking. And what rushed in was Jane, all Jane, his need for her and his desire for her and the hunger that made his bones shake in his body.

He'd turned off the flashlight, and it was pitch-dark in the tent. But he knew the lines and curves of Jane's body better than he knew his own, and as his hands molded themselves to her shoulders, her back, her hips, he wanted to go on touching her forever.

Her breath hitched and turned ragged, and he loved knowing it was because of him. He slid a hand between her thighs and parted them, and when her legs fell open, his fingers found so much heat and wetness that he groaned.

She pushed herself up into his palm and murmured his name. "Caleb . . ."

He stroked and delved until she was writhing beneath him. Only when she begged him—*please, Caleb, please*—did he slide a hand under her thigh to hoist her leg over his hip. Then he pushed inside, slowly, afraid of coming too soon.

He rested his forehead against hers, his whole body rigid with the determination to last until Jane could come with him. He could tell by the heat and pulse of her body, the way she squirmed and moaned and dug her nails into his back, that she was close. He began to move, rocking against her with each thrust.

Then there was no more restraint. They were moving together with fevered intensity, hungry and savage, desperate and wild. They came at the same time, their bodies shuddering with release, and when he collapsed against Jane, he murmured her name over and over, his lips vibrating against her skin.

The cold had been driven away. The warmth they shared felt strong enough to heat the whole world. He rolled onto his side, bringing Jane with him, stroking her hair with one hand as she nestled against his chest.

They fell asleep heartbeat to heartbeat.

◆　◆　◆

Jane woke in a blissful cocoon.

Caleb was all around her. His scent, his skin, his warmth, his strength. Snuggled together inside a double sleeping bag, they couldn't have been any closer, but suddenly it wasn't enough.

She slid her arms around his neck and pressed her lips to his bare chest, just below his collar bone. She tangled her legs with his, rubbing against him like a cat, and she felt him harden as he woke with a rush and a surge, sliding his hands into her hair and pulling her up for a kiss.

Lips and tongue and teeth, hot and wet and carnal. When he slid inside, the friction and fullness almost made her come right then.

He rolled them over so she was on top. She heard someone moaning and realized it was her, and then she remembered they were by themselves on a mountaintop with no one around for miles, and she let herself cry out.

She arched her back and squeezed her muscles tight, and Caleb groaned as he came, his body pulsing inside hers.

In the utter darkness of the tent, it felt like they were alone in the universe, a spark of heat in a cold world. As she slid down Caleb's body to find a nook for her head, his hand stroked her back and he murmured her name.

◆　◆　◆

The next time she woke, it was dawn.

She didn't want to move. She wanted to stay in the circle of Caleb's arms for the rest of her life, no matter how long or short that might be.

But then she remembered that the fog and clouds were gone. She'd watched it happen last night, the stars winking at her as they appeared, one by one, in the velvety darkness.

And now the sun was coming up. She had to go out and look at the view.

She slid carefully out of the sleeping bag, doing her best not to wake Caleb. She pulled on her pants and shirt and jacket and unzipped the tent flap to grab her shoes.

A minute later she was standing outside, the whole world at her feet.

She hadn't known it was possible to see so far. The mountains seemed to stretch out forever in every shade of brown and green, beneath a sky so translucent it was like the inside of a robin's egg. Away to the east, the sun was rising in a glory of colors—coral and rose, tangerine and peach, lilac and violet.

"Now this is what I call a morning."

She turned her head and saw Caleb standing beside her, the scruff of his beard catching the sunlight and his eyes like moss and amber.

"It looks like God does puffed sleeves," she said.

He raised his eyebrows. "Meaning?"

"Well, look at it." She gestured toward the sunrise. "Talk about unnecessary flourishes. I mean, all those colors are just excessive. What useful purpose do they serve, except to be beautiful?"

He slid a hand into her hair and combed through it slowly.

"Okay, you've convinced me. Not everything has to be useful."

They stood there awhile longer, watching the sun make its slow, majestic way above the horizon. Then Caleb spoke.

"Are you ready to say goodbye to Sam?"

She took a deep breath. "Yes."

They carried the urn to the place they'd been yesterday. The wind wasn't as strong, but it was still at their backs, and as they stood there at the edge of the world, Jane imagined Sam's voice whispering to them.

Now that's what I'm talking about.

Knowing this was what Sam had wanted didn't make it any easier. Jane put her hand on the lid of the urn, but she couldn't make herself lift it.

It's all right, Jane. You can do it.

Then Caleb's hand was covering hers. "Will you let me help?"

Tears sprang into her eyes as she nodded. They took off the lid together and set it on the ground, and then they tipped the urn and cast the ashes into the air.

For a moment she saw them, a fine dust scattered on the wind.

And then they were gone.

"Goodbye, Sam," she whispered.

Stay safe, little sis. I love you.

Caleb put an arm around her shoulders, and she leaned against him, his strength like an anchor in a stormy sea. They stood there for a long time.

Then she straightened up and took a deep breath.

"Well," she said. "I guess it's time to hike down this mountain."

On their way back to camp, Jane didn't hear Sam's voice. But she knew, somehow, that her sister was closer than ever.

Before they set out on the return trip, Caleb made oatmeal and hot chocolate for breakfast. Then Jane helped him pack everything up.

The ashes hadn't weighed that much, but when she put on her pack, the urn inside seemed as light as a feather.

"You should give me something more to carry," she said to Caleb, watching him hoist his big pack onto his shoulders. "This isn't a fair division of labor."

He smiled at her. "Don't worry about me, tenderfoot. We've got a long hike ahead of us."

She supposed it was long, but it felt easy. Going down was a lot less stressful than going up, especially with perfect weather and the trekking poles to absorb the shock when the trail was steep. They stopped at the shelter where they'd drunk coffee the day before, and while they munched on protein bars, Jane swung her feet like a little kid.

"Jane."

"Yes?"

Caleb had been thoughtful on the hike down, even distracted. A few times when she'd called out to him it had taken more than one try to get his attention. Now, as she turned to look at him, his expression was serious.

A moment went by.

"What?" she asked finally, her curiosity growing.

"I want you to come to Australia with me."

She stared at him. What, exactly, was he asking her?

"You mean . . . like for a visit? When you go back?"

He shook his head. "I mean for as long as I'm there. I want you to live with me, Jane."

She was so stunned she didn't know what to say.

"But . . ." She struggled to form a coherent sentence. "But you wouldn't even stay with me for Christmas."

Not exactly the most important point right now, but it's what her brain came up with.

"I know. And I've regretted it ever since." He reached out and took her hand. "I think you'd love Australia. It's beautiful."

After what they'd shared during the last forty-eight hours, Jane knew her feelings for Caleb ran deeper than friendship and physical attraction. There was something else there, too—something she'd never expected. Something that made her weak in the knees when she looked at him, and not just because he turned her on so damn much.

So why wasn't she happier that Caleb had invited her to Australia?

She bit her lip. "It means a lot to me that you asked. Honestly. But . . . have you thought this through?"

He frowned a little. "What do you mean?"

When he held her hand and gazed into her eyes, he was pretty much irresistible. He hadn't said he loved her, or asked her to marry him, or talked about how long he wanted them to be together, but this was a pretty big first step.

So why did it feel wrong?

"You want me to just . . ." She gestured toward the ridge, as though Australia were beyond it. "Pack up my things and go to the other side of the world?"

He raised an eyebrow. "They have stores in Australia, you know. You don't have to pack much. I'm a big believer in traveling light."

"I know you are." She took a breath. "But I don't travel light. I own a bookstore, for one thing. How am I supposed to travel with that?"

"Hire someone to manage it while you're gone. New York can still be your home base."

How could she explain to him that it wasn't just what she did for a living, but how she liked to live? And the fact that he didn't seem to be taking that into account?

"I've got at least a hundred books I wouldn't want to be without. Do you know how much a hundred books weigh?"

"Get the e-book versions and read them on your phone."

"Some of them are signed copies or rare editions. Some of them are from my childhood, the first books I fell in love with. Reading them is a tactile experience. E-books aren't the same."

He sighed. "Okay, fine. You can ship them." His gaze slid down her body, and even with the bulky layers of clothing between them, her skin tingled as though he'd touched her bare skin. "Especially if you read naked."

She smiled in spite of herself. "What would I do while you were off on your expeditions? Besides read naked."

There was a spark in his hazel eyes. "You'd be with me."

Okay, she hadn't expected that.

"I see," she said slowly. "So I'd be trekking with you, hiking and white-water rafting and climbing mountains."

"I watched you up on that summit, Jane. You're a natural."

"That was the most amazing thing I've ever done in my life. But—"

His face lit up. "That was only the beginning. We'll go around the world together. Places you can't even imagine."

"But that's not how I want to live."

Silence.

Then: "What do you mean?"

She sighed. "You liked *Anne of Green Gables*, right? But that doesn't mean you suddenly want to be a children's librarian. I loved hiking with you, Caleb—but that doesn't mean I want to live like that."

She saw the disbelief in his eyes. "But I saw your face this morning. I've never seen you look so happy."

"I don't think I've ever been that happy. I'd climbed a mountain for the first time in my life, and the view was like something from heaven. I felt closer to Sam than I ever have before, and I said goodbye to her. And you and I . . ." Her body tingled again as she remembered. "And you and I made love. So yes, I was happy. But that doesn't mean I want to be your hiking partner. I can't step into Sam's shoes."

His brows drew together. "I would never expect you to. That's not what I want."

"What *do* you want?"

"To be with you." He looked frustrated. "Don't you want that, too? You don't have to go on expeditions with me—not all of them, anyway. Not at first. We'll get a place."

"A place," she repeated slowly. "And what would I do there?"

"Anything you want."

"Could I open a bookstore?"

He frowned. "That wouldn't be practical."

"Why not?"

"We wouldn't be in Australia for that long," he said, his voice defensive.

"How long?"

"Well . . . I have expeditions scheduled through July."

"And then?"

He made a wide sweep with his hand, as though encompassing the whole world. "Wherever you want. Europe, Asia, South America."

She thought about that. "Wherever *you* want, you mean."

"No. It can be your choice. Sometimes we'll go where the business is, of course. But most of the time I plan expeditions where I want to go, and people will pay to come along." He paused. "This time we'll plan where *we* want to go."

A part of her was tempted. But—

"I'm not saying I don't ever want to travel. I would like to. But, Caleb . . . my life in New York isn't just a default setting. It's the life I've built for myself. It's part of who I am."

He was looking at her like he couldn't believe what she was saying. "Living in one place like that, in a city—" He shook his head. "Your life could be so much bigger than that, Jane. *You* could be bigger."

And with those words, a wave of coldness went through her.

What had tempted her wasn't the life he'd described, but Caleb himself. Her feelings for him were so overwhelming that it would be easy to say yes, to give up everything and go with him, follow him anywhere, just so she could be near him.

But if he thought her life was small—if he thought *she* was small for living that life—then he didn't really value her. The life he was describing was based on what *he* valued. He wanted her to be part of it, but he didn't want his own life to change at all.

She stood up abruptly. "Let's go. It's only forty-five minutes from here, right?"

"Jane—"

She picked up her trekking poles. "I don't want to talk anymore right now."

Chapter Twenty

As they hiked the rest of the way down the mountain, Caleb's frustration continued to grow.

Last December, Jane had said the mistake women made with him was believing they were special. Different. They slept with him and started thinking about the future.

Well, Jane was special. She was different. And he did want a future with her.

She just didn't want one with him.

He couldn't understand it. That incredible night in December might have been a one-time thing, passion brought about by shared grief and long-suppressed attraction. But last night?

Whatever was between him and Jane, it was there to stay. She had to know that, too. Didn't she?

But if she did, why had she rejected him?

When they reached the car, he put their packs in the trunk and slid into the driver's seat. Jane settled into the passenger seat next to him, and her deep sigh told him she was enjoying the comfort of a car more than she ever had before.

He started the engine and pulled out of the lot.

"This is a first for me, you know," he said abruptly.

She looked at him. "What is?"

"Asking a woman to travel with me."

She didn't answer right away, and he had time to replay his words and wonder if they'd sounded as arrogant to her as they did in his head.

"I have a first for you," she said after a moment.

"What?"

"Move in with me. Live with me in Brooklyn." She paused. "I've never asked a man that before."

Was she serious?

"You know I can't do that."

"Why not?"

"It's not practical. Not with my work."

He'd asked her to make adjustments to her work, too. But this was different.

Wasn't it?

"You can stay with me between expeditions. I'll be your home base."

He frowned out at the road in front of him. "I'd rather live where I'm trekking, like I'm doing now in Australia. It makes more sense. And I don't want a part-time relationship. I want you with me, damn it. Are we going to talk about this seriously or not?"

"I was trying to," she said, and she sounded so reasonable he felt ashamed.

"I'm sorry," he said gruffly. "I don't mean to . . ."

"Sound like an asshole?"

"Yeah."

"That's all right."

It's because I want you. Because I don't want to travel without you. Because I love you.

Maybe if he told her that, everything else would work out. But she had to know how he felt. He'd told her last night, sort of.

If there aren't any answers, what is there?

People who love you.

She had to know he'd been talking about himself. Didn't she?

Of course, he could take away any doubt by telling her now.

I love you, Jane.

But he'd already been rejected once today. If he told her he loved her, and she rejected him again?

His hands tightened on the steering wheel, and they drove the rest of the way to the motel in silence.

He pulled into the parking lot and turned off the engine. Then he did his best to shift gears into practicality.

"Do you want to take a shower while I check us out?"

She nodded gratefully. "I would love to take a shower. Even one with no water pressure."

"All right, then. Let's meet back here in fifteen minutes."

The final stage of their journey started the way the last leg had ended: in silence.

After an hour, Caleb couldn't take it anymore.

"So we're really going to Prince Edward Island."

Jane turned to look at him, startled.

"Of course. I mean . . . that was always the plan. Wasn't it?"

"Yeah." He kept his eyes on the road. "I guess I thought your plans might have changed after last night, but I was obviously wrong. You still want to go meet that guy."

"It's not . . ." She shook her head. "It's not like that. You know it's not. This isn't a date, Caleb. And it's Sam he wrote the letter to."

He knew he was worrying at a sore spot that wasn't the real source of his pain, but he couldn't seem to stop himself. "You called him your ideal man. Don't you remember? The day you first met him."

She stared at him. "I don't believe it. After everything that's happened since then, you think I have some romantic fantasy about Dan?"

"Don't you?"

"No! This trip isn't even about him. Not really. It's about Sam and fixing a mistake I made."

"But after last night—"

"The two things don't have anything to do with each other. I can't leave Dan standing on a bridge all alone, waiting for a woman who won't come."

His jaw tightened. "Jesus. He's not going to be there, Jane."

"Why are you so sure of that? Are you really so cynical about people?"

He glanced at her for a second. "Yeah," he said. "I guess I am."

Silence fell between them again. On either side, Canadian forest stretched as far as the eye could see.

This time, it was Jane who broke the silence.

"Are we going to talk any more about my idea?"

"What idea?"

"You moving in with me. Using Brooklyn as your home base between expeditions."

Part of him knew that what she was offering was a compromise, but it felt like a rejection.

"A long-distance relationship, huh?"

She nodded. "Isn't that better than no relationship?"

He felt a familiar frustration: not being able to put his thoughts and feelings into words. Not the way Jane could.

"It's not what I want."

"What do you want?"

"I want you with me."

God, he sounded petulant. But damn it, that *was* what he wanted.

Jane didn't say anything else, and there was another long stretch of silence between them.

"You'd think I'd have figured this out before now," he muttered after a while.

"What?"

"Opposites might attract, but they don't work. Not for the long haul. All they do is hurt each other."

Jane was quiet for a moment.

"You're talking about your parents," she said, not asking.

"Yeah. I guess."

"What about my parents?"

"What do you mean?"

"They're different, too. And they've made it work for thirty-five years of marriage."

He felt his jaw tightening. "I can't live in Brooklyn."

"Of course you can. You just don't want to."

Anger shot through him. "Well, the same is true for you, isn't it? You *could* come to Australia and be with me. You just don't want to."

After a minute, Jane shrugged. "So . . . stalemate, then."

"I guess so."

And even though it was the inevitable conclusion, he was filled with regret and the ache of loss.

So he put on country music, the time-honored choice for people in pain.

"This is the only kind of music I absolutely hate," Jane grumbled.

"Too bad," he said. "You can suck it up."

She gave him a sideways glance. "Or we could talk about finding some middle ground."

He shook his head. "You were the one who called it a stalemate. Anyway, it won't do any good. Let's give it a rest." He paused. "We should change the subject. How many kids did Anne and Gilbert have?"

They stuck to noncontroversial topics for the rest of the trip. Jane fell asleep for a long stretch of the Trans-Canada Highway, waking up only when they reached the bridge that would take them over the water to Prince Edward Island.

"Where are we? Are we there?" she asked, rubbing her eyes and muffling a yawn.

She was adorable when she yawned, and he felt a pang. The truth was, he found every damn thing she did adorable.

"Almost," he said. "This is the Confederation Bridge. Once we're across it we'll be on the island. It's another half hour to Cavendish."

She checked her watch. "We'll get there forty minutes before sunset," she said, sounding pleased.

"Yep."

He sounded sour, and he gave himself a mental shake. He could keep on punishing Jane for not wanting what he wanted, or he could get himself together and start acting like a man.

When they reached the island and began to drive north, through rolling farmland and sparkling ponds and little wooded hills, it was easier to be cheerful.

Jane rolled down her window and stared out at the countryside.

"I can't believe it. Oh, Caleb, it's so beautiful."

It really was. The fields were covered with wildflowers, flowering trees were laden with blossoms, and the deep blue sky made everything seem brighter.

"The roads are even red," she said. "Just like in the book. Remember Anne and Matthew talking about that?"

He did. L. M. Montgomery hadn't provided an explanation, but the naturalist in him had been curious, and he'd Googled it.

"The color comes from iron-oxide in the soil," he said, but he wasn't sure Jane heard him. She was gazing out the window, and her eyes were full of visions.

As the sun sank lower behind them, the scenes they drove through were drenched in gold. The mellow light seemed to illuminate every leaf and twig and blade of grass.

When they entered Cavendish, he started to pay closer attention to the directions on his phone. Navigation was pretty simple—there was one main thoroughfare through the town—and soon they were turning right into a narrow road that led to a national park. The ocean and red sandstone cliffs were on the left; a grassy lane through fields and trees was on the right. Ahead in that direction he caught a glimpse of blue.

"The Lake of Shining Waters," Jane breathed.

There were a few cars in the parking lot, but tourist season wouldn't start until June and it wasn't crowded. He pulled into a spot near the lane and turned off the car.

He looked over at Jane. She was smiling, her face full of anticipation, and he'd never felt farther away from her or more incapable of telling her what he was feeling.

The island was beautiful. More beautiful than he'd imagined. And Jane was right—it really was like the book they'd listened to. There was a magic in that, especially for her, and all he wanted to do was share that with her.

He'd give anything if they could have come here for a different reason. Not for Horn-Rims, but just for themselves.

If they were here for themselves, they could wander along the red sand beaches and wade in the ocean and kiss whenever they felt like it. They could stay in a white clapboard inn surrounded by gardens, with rocking chairs on the porch and fireplaces in the bedroom, and they could make love all night long.

And right now, the glow on Jane's face would be because the two of them were about to go out and discover the Lake of Shining Waters together.

"I shouldn't be so excited," she said. "I'm the bearer of bad news, after all. But it's incredible to be here after loving Anne for so many years, and I can't help looking forward to this walk." She glanced at her watch. "Half an hour till sunset. He might be there already, though. I'm going to go now."

"He won't be there."

When Jane looked at him, some of the pleasure was gone from her expression.

Guilt tugged at him. *I'm sorry,* he wanted to say, but the words didn't come.

When she spoke, her voice was stiff. "Do you want to come with me?" she asked. "To oversee your bet?"

It took him a moment to remember what she was talking about. Damn, he'd forgotten all about that.

"That's all right," he said. "I trust you." He paused, and then he forced himself to speak again. "I'll wait here. Good luck, Jane."

"Thanks." She gave him a half smile, and then she was out the door, walking toward the grassy lane, her face toward the sunset.

He watched her go. Back at the motel she'd changed into jeans and a long-sleeved cotton shirt, the same dark blue as her eyes. Her long brown braid swung as she walked. She was wearing sandals instead of her muddy sneakers, and he wondered if her feet hurt from yesterday's hike.

If so, she didn't show it. She was tougher than she looked.

But she was in for a disappointment when Horn-Rims failed to show up for their meeting.

Maybe it had been a mistake not to go with her. He could keep her company until it got dark, and when she finally acknowledged that the man she'd built up as some kind of romantic hero was just an ordinary asshole, he'd be there for her.

And then, maybe, they could have the trip he'd fantasized about. A few days together away from everything. A way to say goodbye before they went their separate ways.

Or even to convince Jane to come with him, after all.

He got out of the car and went after her.

The lane curved through stands of spruce trees and little meadows, blowing grasses and flowering shrubs. Then it came around a bend to give a clear view of the Lake of Shining Waters, sparkling in the setting sun as though it were covered in diamonds.

The sun was in his line of vision, and he used his hand to shade his eyes. Jane was fifty yards ahead of him on the path, heading toward a small wooden bridge where . . .

He stopped.

There was a man standing on the bridge with his back to them, leaning over the railing and watching the geese and ducks drifting past. It was hard to tell from here, but he thought—

The man turned and saw Jane.

Jane started to walk faster, and by the time she reached him she was practically running. He'd started forward to meet her and held out his arms, and then they were hugging like long-lost siblings.

Or lovers.

A vise was squeezing his heart. This was what he'd been afraid of— that Jane's romantic fantasies would somehow come to life and take her away from him. That what she wanted from him he could never give, and that what he could give her would never be enough.

He was a cynic when it came to people, and he had no interest in fairy tales. He wanted real life, the natural world, and he wanted Jane with him. But she lived in a world of stories, of dreams, and even if his job didn't take him around the world and away from her, he could never be the hero she wanted.

He didn't think Dan could be, either. Sam was the sister he'd fallen for. But watching them together at the Lake of Shining Waters, he remembered the day in Jane's shop when the two of them had bonded over a book.

Jane thought of Dan as a kindred spirit. And in spite of everything she and Caleb had shared on this trip, she would never see him that way.

He couldn't watch anymore. He'd always thought he had a high tolerance for pain, but it turned out he was wrong. Because no matter who Jane ended up with someday, it wouldn't be him, and he was getting a preview right now of what that would feel like.

It hurt like hell. It hurt like nothing he'd ever felt before.

And there was no way he was sticking around for it.

He turned and went back the way he came, and when he got back to the car, he pulled out his phone and started making calls.

Chapter Twenty-One

Jane told Dan what had happened to Samantha, and she told him what she'd done—creating an imaginary woman with her personality in Sam's body. Dan was kind and understanding, and obviously very sorry to hear about Sam's death, but he didn't seem like a man who'd just learned that his dream woman had not only died, but had never really existed in the first place.

"Can I ask you something?" Jane ventured.

They'd gone to sit on a wooden bench not far from the bridge, with a view of the lake and the sunset.

"Of course," Dan said, turning to face her.

He was the same charming, handsome man she remembered—but how could she have thought she was attracted to him? Compared to Caleb, he was like a pale shadow. Dan was intelligent, pleasant, good-looking . . . but Caleb shook her to her very core.

Of course Dan hadn't been attracted to her, either. It was Sam he'd fallen for.

Hadn't he?

"I was just wondering. After I read your letter, I thought you might really be in love with Sam. But now it seems like . . ." She trailed off.

It took him a moment to answer. He looked out over the lake and then back at her.

"I did believe what I wrote in that letter. Not just at the time, but for a few months afterward. But there were other things going on in my life, too. Things I didn't tell you about." He paused. "My wife and I separated last summer. She'd moved out of our house just three months before I met you. Looking back, it seems obvious that I was struggling to deal with that, which had a lot to do with the way I reacted to Sam. But it's hard to see your own emotions when you're in them."

"I can definitely relate to that," Jane said wryly.

He hesitated. "There's something I should admit to you. Something I should have seen at the time, and which I'm not proud of."

"What?"

He looked embarrassed. "The fact is . . . well . . . your sister strongly resembled my wife."

Jane stared at him. "She did?"

"Not in the way she looked, but in her spirit. Her vitality." He pulled out his wallet and showed her a picture. "That's Julia."

She studied the photo for a minute. This woman was small, with dark hair and skin. Superficially, at least, the two women were very different. But the sparkle in their eyes was the same, along with their big grins and joyful expressions.

Dan put his wallet back in his pocket. "My feelings for your sister had little to do with her and everything to do with my wife. I mapped all sorts of fantasies onto Samantha—especially after you told me about her . . . or, well, you," he added with a smile. "That made the resemblance seem stronger. My ex-wife's taste in literature is much like yours."

"So neither Sam was real," Jane murmured. "Not the one I created or the one you imagined."

He shook his head. "I'm afraid not. I realized about a month ago what I'd done, and I finally found the courage to talk to Julia about the problems that led to our divorce. We've been talking ever since."

219

"I'm glad," she said.

"That's kind of you." He paused. "Once I came to my senses, I was sure Samantha wouldn't be at the bridge today. Why would she travel so far to meet a total stranger? But if she did, I couldn't let her wait for a man who would never appear. So I came." He smiled at her. "And here you are, for the same reason."

"I thought it was my fault. I mean, if I hadn't told you all those things about Sam, you wouldn't have written that letter. Or so I thought. And I couldn't let you wait for her and wonder . . ."

"I understand."

"That wasn't the only reason I came, though."

"What was your other reason?"

The sun had dropped below the horizon, and the light was fading. For now, though, color clung to the puffed clouds on the horizon.

"I made up a version of Sam that didn't exist. I wanted . . . it seemed important . . ." She groped for words. "I needed to tell you the truth."

He nodded slowly. "Why do you think that was so important to you?"

How could she explain it?

She took a breath. "When we were kids, there were times I made Sam into a villain in my mind because we were so different, or because I was jealous of her. And even after we grew up, there were whole parts of her life I didn't understand or know much about. And then, after she died . . . I sort of did the opposite. I created this kind of idealized version of her. Caleb—the man who brought me here—keeps reminding me that she wasn't a saint. That she was human. He helped me to get to know the real Sam again. The sister I loved." She bit her lip. "That's the Sam I wish I'd told you about."

Dan looked at her for a moment. Then he got to his feet and held out a hand to help her up.

"So tell me now," he said.

She stood up beside him. "Tell you . . . ?"

"About Sam. I'd like to know. We can walk along the lake, if you like. It's beautiful with the evening coming on."

And so she and Dan walked beside the Lake of Shining Waters, and she talked to him about her sister.

She told him about Sam as a child and as a teenager. She told him about Sam's hike up Owl Mountain, when she'd decided she wanted to be a wilderness leader, and how she'd wanted her ashes scattered there. She told him about Caleb, too, and the business they'd started together.

"She loved what she did. She was so full of life. More than anyone I know, except for Caleb. That's why it seemed so . . . so wrong when she died. Like it couldn't be. For a long time I just couldn't accept it. It took me a long time to say goodbye."

"And now?"

"I've said goodbye. But the funny thing is, now that I've made that peace, it doesn't feel like she's gone." She put a hand on her heart. "It feels like she's here."

◆ ◆ ◆

On their way back to the bridge, they talked about other things. His life, and hers, and the strange confluence of events that had brought them so briefly together. She didn't realize how much she'd also talked about Caleb until Dan said, "Your boyfriend sounds like a remarkable man."

"My—oh no," she said quickly. "Caleb's not my boyfriend." She blinked. "I didn't mean that in a bad way. Any woman would be lucky to have him. He's the kindest, most generous, most decent man I've ever known."

"Ah."

She glanced at him. "You put a lot of meaning into that *Ah*."

He smiled. "All right, then, I'll be more direct." He paused. "Don't repeat the mistakes that brought both of us here."

"What mistakes?"

"Don't miss the person standing right in front of you. And don't fail to look into your own heart, no matter how difficult it might be."

They were almost back where they'd started. They went the rest of the way in silence, and as they walked, she thought about Caleb. She thought about last December at her apartment, and last night on the mountain, and sitting in the car in the dark, listening to *Anne of Green Gables*.

They were back at the bridge. She leaned over the railing, looking down into the twilight-gray waters, but what she saw was Caleb's face.

He was so stubborn. He'd rejected the very idea of finding middle ground. Why was he so determined to bring her with him on his adventures around the world instead of trying to see if they could make a long-distance relationship work?

Why wouldn't he compromise?

She'd been proud of herself for being so reasonable, for controlling the part of herself that was willing to give up anything, to follow him anywhere, just for the chance to be with him. But why couldn't Caleb understand that was no foundation for a relationship? Why couldn't *he* be reasonable?

Then she thought about his parents, and her heart clenched. How much damage had his mother and father, with their very different desertions, done to him?

She remembered what he'd said when they got back to the car that morning—that asking a woman to travel with him was a first. She hadn't given him any credit for that. But for Caleb, it really was a big deal.

He'd structured his life so he could be alone without being lonely—out in nature by himself, or leading groups of adventurers.

He'd never committed to a woman before. Then, when he finally wanted to, his instinct was to grab on too tight—and not give up any part of his own life.

He was afraid. But in spite of that, he wanted to be with her. He was hanging in there.

She thought about the way he'd made her feel that night in December and last night on the mountain. If there was no such thing as speech, if she had only body language to go on, how would she think Caleb felt about her?

Her heart started to pound. "I need to talk to him."

"Your friend?"

She'd almost forgotten Dan was there. "Yes."

He nodded gently. "That sounds like a good idea."

She started off down the lane, realized she hadn't said goodbye, and came rushing back. "Good luck with your wife," she said breathlessly. "I hope you guys work things out."

"Thank you, Jane. And thank you for the walk." He made a shooing motion with his hand. "Now go."

The light was almost gone. She broke into a run halfway down the lane, so eager to reach Caleb that she stumbled twice.

She burst into the parking lot, looked around, and stopped cold. Where was Caleb? Had he gone somewhere? When would he be back?

Most of the other cars in the lot had gone. But a few remained, along with a taxi parked not far from where Caleb's car had been. As she stood there wondering what to do next, the taxi driver emerged from his cab.

"Jane Finch?"

She stared at him. "Yes, that's me."

"I've got your suitcase in the trunk. I've been hired by Caleb Bryce to take you anywhere you want to go."

She didn't understand. "Is he all right?" A clutch of panic. "Is he on the way to the hospital or something?"

"He seemed fine when I saw him. He told me to tell you he'd sent you an email."

An email. Maybe there'd been a family emergency—his brother or his aunt. But if so, why hadn't he called her? She fumbled in her purse for her phone, glad now she'd gotten an international data plan, and opened her email.

> Jane,
> Since you made it very clear that our lives will never mesh, I figured I wouldn't waste any time getting out of yours.
> You won the bet, which means I owe you a thousand dollars. I've hired this taxi to take you anywhere you want, whether to a hotel or the Charlottetown airport or all the way back to New York. I'll pay for your hotel, and if you decide to take a plane back, I'll pay for your ticket.
> Caleb

That was it. That was all he had to say to her.

She reread the short paragraphs with growing fury.

God, what an idiot she was.

She'd told herself he wanted to be with her. That he was hanging tough even though he was afraid.

She'd thought she knew how he really felt. She'd told herself to listen to his body language.

How was this for body language? He'd actually run away from her.

It turned out that a man could make love to you like you were the most important, most precious thing in the universe and still take off the next day.

And this wasn't even the first time. He'd taken off in December, too.

Well, at least she could be sure of something this time. This would be the last morning-after the two of them shared, and the last time he had a chance to run out on her.

"That bastard. That *bastard!*"

The taxi driver looked startled.

"The gentleman who hired me?" he asked cautiously.

She wanted to kick something. But the only thing available was this guy's tire, and that would be a lousy way to start off what was, apparently, going to be a longer relationship than anything she and Caleb could manage.

"He's not a gentleman, and yes." She took a deep breath. "And I'm not taking a cent of his money. How did he hire you? Did he leave a credit card on file?"

"Yes, he did, with unlimited authorization."

She pulled out her wallet, fished out her bank card, and handed it to him. "Cancel it and take mine instead." She took another breath. "It looks like I'll be staying here overnight. Where's the nearest hotel?"

It was dark by the time Caleb hit the Trans-Canada Highway again, but his mood was darker.

Jane had read his email by now. He'd written it in a tangle of emotion, anger at himself and anger at her and anger at the goddamn universe for making him fall in love when he didn't have a clue how to deal with it.

His hands tightened on the steering wheel. He'd written to Jane in the heat of jealousy and bitterness and fear, and he already regretted it.

He regretted it, but he was glad it was too late to take it back. Because they didn't belong together. They lived in different worlds, and all they could bring each other was misery and the slow wrenching away of two people trying and failing to make things work.

His phone buzzed, and when he saw Jane's name on the screen, he almost swerved into oncoming traffic.

He forced himself to wait until it was safe to pull onto the shoulder. Then he put on his hazard lights, took a deep breath, and read Jane's text.

As it turned out, there was more than one.

You son of a bitch.

I always knew you were a coward, but I never thought you'd literally run away from me.

I hope you get bitten by every insect in Australia. I hope a kangaroo kicks you in the head.

If you think you can buy your way out of this, think again.

I gave the taxi driver my card instead of yours. I won't be taking a single penny from you.

And don't bother trying to call me, because I'm blocking your number on my phone. And don't bother trying to email, because I've rerouted anything coming from you to my spam folder.

That's where you belong, Caleb. The spam folder of life.

I hope I never see you again.

His hand tightened on the phone. He could practically see her in front of him, her arms folded and her eyes spitting fire, and her words etched in fury.

And all he could think about was how much he loved her.

Shit.

Shit, shit, shit.

It's too late, he reminded himself as he pulled back onto the highway. *It's too late to un-fuck this. But Jane will be okay, because she's the most incredible woman in the world, and she's going to meet someone a hundred times better than you.*

And for the rest of his life, whenever he saw something beautiful, he would think of her.

An hour later his phone buzzed again, and he experienced a moment of feverish hope before he saw the name on the screen.

Hunter.

Right. He'd promised to phone his brother so they could figure out a joint visit to Rosemary this summer. Maybe he should stop somewhere for dinner and give him a call.

As he thought that, a wave of bone-deep fatigue went through his body. In the last three days he'd driven for eighteen hours, hiked for six, and camped on a mountaintop. He hadn't gotten much sleep, and if he didn't want to cause an accident on this godforsaken highway, he'd better think about stopping somewhere, not just for dinner but for the night.

There was a chain hotel twenty minutes down the road. It was overpriced, but it would have room service, and that sounded damn good right now.

He checked in, placed a dinner order, and called Hunter while he was waiting for it.

"Sorry I didn't phone."

"Don't worry about it. I knew you were going to Maine and Canada with Jane. How's the trip?"

If he had a week, he might be able to answer that question.

"Fine. We scattered Sam's ashes, which was the important thing. Jane's still on Prince Edward Island. I think she'll probably stay there for a day or two."

"You think? Don't you know?"

"We, uh, had a parting of the ways. I'm on my way back to New York now."

There was a short silence.

"A parting of the ways? What does that mean?"

"Jane found what she was looking for, and she didn't really need me around anymore."

Another silence.

"Caleb, you sound like shit. What's really going on?"

He sighed long and deep. "How much time have you got?"

So he told Hunter the whole story—the night at Jane's apartment and everything that had happened since. His dinner came when he was halfway through, but his brother didn't seem to mind that he talked with his mouth full.

"So that's that," he said when he was finished. "It's pretty fucking ironic, if you think about it. I was always so afraid of turning into Dad, you know? I made my life as different from his as I could. Dad spent his life stuck in one place, and I travel around the world. Dad had the ranch and all those burdens he couldn't deal with, and I'm fancy-free. He fell in love with a woman who gave him hell, and I swore I'd never fall in love. And now here I am."

"Yeah. Here you are." Hunter paused. "But it isn't Dad you turned into. It's Mom."

Caleb froze. "What the hell are you talking about?"

"Can't you see it? Wandering around the world, determined never to be tied down. And walking out on the best thing that ever happened to you."

"You mean . . . Jane?"

"Of course I mean Jane. Jesus Christ, Caleb. I've never heard you talk about anything the way you spent the last hour talking about that woman. You're head over heels in love with her, out of your mind crazy about her, and you left her in a parking lot."

He was starting to wish he hadn't eaten so much.

"We don't belong together," he said gruffly. "It would never work. You saw what happened to Mom and Dad."

"Caleb. You're not Dad, and in spite of the dick move you pulled today, you're not Mom, either. Your life worked fine when you weren't in love, but now you are. So you're going to have to make some adjustments."

Caleb closed his eyes. "You make it sound so simple. But you don't know Jane."

"I met her once. She seemed pretty fucking fantastic, to be honest."

"She is. But she's a romantic. She's got this big imagination. She's always dreaming up ideal people. I'll never be able to live up to that."

"That sounds like your own fear talking, not Jane. And you can't love an ideal person. That's hollow. Empty and cold. It takes real love from a real person to keep you warm."

To keep you warm.

All he'd ever wanted was to keep Jane warm. He wanted to keep her warm and safe and loved, and he wanted to do it for the rest of his life.

But he'd fucked up his chance to do that, and he'd fucked it up good.

"It's too late."

He didn't realize he'd said that out loud until Hunter answered him.

"What do you mean, it's too late?"

"It's too late to fix things with Jane. I really screwed up."

Hunter was quiet for a moment. "Yeah, you did. But if you get off your ass, it's not too late to fix it."

That was a bossy older brother for you. "It's not, huh? Why do you think that?"

"Because you're both alive. As long as you're alive, you can fix anything." He paused. "Make a gesture."

"A gesture?"

"Yeah. Some kind of big gesture to show her how you feel. Women like that."

"I question your expertise in this area. When was your last serious relationship?"

"It's been a while. But at least I've actually had one. In the land of the blind, the one-eyed man is king."

For a long time after they hung up, Caleb thought about Hunter's words.

As long as you're alive, you can fix anything.

Was his brother right?

There was only one way to find out.

Chapter Twenty-Two

Jane stayed on Prince Edward Island for three days.

She was very glad she hadn't flown straight home. By the time she woke up on the third day, she was feeling much calmer and less like tracking Caleb down and killing him.

The hotel she stayed at was right next door to the *Anne of Green Gables* museum. This was the actual nineteenth-century farmhouse that had inspired L. M. Montgomery, and it looked just as she'd described in the book. It was surrounded by fields and gardens and the woodland paths that had given rise to Lover's Lane and the Haunted Wood and all the other places Anne had walked.

She spent a whole day wandering those paths, breathing the moss-scented air and looking for wildflowers and listening to the little brook that danced over polished rocks . . . and remembering the quotes Caleb had showed her.

It has always seemed to me that, amid all the commonplaces of life, I was very near to a kingdom of ideal beauty. Between it and me hung only a thin veil. I could never quite draw it aside, but sometimes a wind fluttered it and I caught a glimpse of the enchanting world beyond—only a glimpse, but those glimpses have always made life worthwhile.

The house itself was furnished as it would have been during Anne's time, and it was filled with little touches that evoked the book—a broken slate, and Marilla's amethyst brooch, and a dress made of "soft brown gloria with all the gloss of silk"—and, of course, with the all-important puffed sleeves.

Jane stood in the doorway of Anne's gable bedroom for a long time, looking at the dress hanging on the closet door and thinking of the picture she'd shown Caleb.

Everything she saw made her think of Caleb.

He was everywhere. When she went walking along the ocean and saw the seagulls wheeling over the red sandstone cliffs, she thought about how much he would have loved that scene. And when she went out one night and ate her fill of fresh mussels and lobster, she wished he were there to taste it with her.

No, you don't, she told herself quickly. *He's the jerk who left you alone in a foreign land.*

A foreign land where people spoke English and everyone was friendly, but still. You needed a passport to get here, and that meant it was a foreign land.

She tried to feel cheerful on the plane ride home. In spite of the mess with Caleb, it had been an incredible trip. She'd said goodbye to Sam, and she'd seen beautiful places she'd only ever imagined.

And before the whole abandoning-her-in-a-parking-lot thing, Caleb had been the best part of the journey.

His body had left some kind of imprint on hers. When she lay in bed at night, she could feel him—his bare skin and the hard muscle beneath and the fierce urgency of his need for her.

No man had ever wanted her so much. Until, of course, he didn't anymore.

Three days had gone by since the night at the Lake of Shining Waters. As much as she wanted to blame Caleb for everything that had gone wrong, the truth was, she'd been the one to reject him first. She'd told him no when he asked her to travel with him.

But she hadn't meant that to be the end of the conversation. She'd wanted to find a way to make things work. He was the one who'd run away, not her. If she couldn't count on him to stick around when things got hard, how could she trust him with her heart?

Not that it mattered now. He must be back in Australia by this time. He'd made it clear he'd had enough of her, and she'd told him never to call or write or see her ever again.

So much for trying to be cheerful.

She wished she hadn't told Kiki and Felicia that she'd go from the airport to the bookstore. But she'd said she would work for a few hours, and they'd be expecting her. Besides, she wasn't really that tired.

Just a little sad.

It was raining in New York, which at least had the advantage of being appropriate to her mood. The taxi ride through the downpour was depressing, especially when she contrasted it with the last time it had rained this hard—when she and Caleb had hiked up Owl Mountain.

It was a slow, quiet afternoon at the Bookworm Turns, with no need for three people to be manning the store. But Kiki and Felicia both stayed until closing, wanting all the details of her trip. She focused on the hike up the mountain and her stay on Prince Edward Island, even though she had a feeling that what her employees really wanted to hear about was Caleb.

They were going for a drink after work and invited her along, but she declined with thanks. She thought about taking a taxi home, but she was craving deli corned beef and her favorite place was around the corner. She'd stop there first and decide if she wanted to take a cab or wheel her suitcase onto the subway.

She put on the rain jacket Caleb had bought for her, which of course made her think of him, and set out for the deli.

On her way, she passed her favorite boutique.

Wear this and you'll find him:
The man of your dreams.

Just like that day in October, the sign brought her up short.

It was the same dress. This display window had been changed out three or four times since the fall, but now here it was again.

She stood in the rain, staring at the dress and remembering what Caleb had said about it the night he'd walked her to the subway.

It's the color of your eyes.

She stared a moment longer. Then she checked the store hours on the door, saw they were open, and went inside.

"May I help you?"

The employee who came forward looked happy to see her, which, considering she was dripping all over the hardwood floors, was very nice.

"I'm sorry about the water," she said apologetically. "I was just wondering about the dress in the window. The blue silk? I remember seeing it last October, but I thought it was gone since then."

The employee, a tall redhead, looked enthusiastic.

"The Alia Montero design? We debuted it here, and it went on to win an Indie Fashion award. So we brought it back for a return engagement, so to speak. We only have it in a few sizes, though." She looked Jane over with experienced eyes. "Six?"

"Yes, but I—"

"You have to try it on," the woman said firmly. "With your coloring and figure, it'll be perfect."

And so Jane found herself in the dressing room, stripping down to her underwear and trying on the blue silk dress.

She was still staring at herself in the mirror when the red-haired employee knocked on the door.

"Mind if I take a look?" She stuck her head in without waiting for an answer. "Oh my goodness, that's lovely. It's like it was made for you." She smiled. "Maybe you'll find the man of your dreams."

And just like that, Jane burst into tears.

"I'm fine," she said to the anxious saleswoman, wiping her eyes with the back of her hand. "Don't mind me. It's just . . . the dress is so beautiful." She gulped past the lump in her throat. "As soon as I change, I'll bring it out to the register."

The other woman looked a little doubtful, but she retreated from the dressing room. "You must really love fashion," she murmured as she closed the door behind her.

Maybe you'll find the man of your dreams.

She'd already found him, Jane thought as she slipped out of the dress and back into her damp clothes. Caleb Bryce was the man of her dreams.

But he'd never told her he loved her. If they were meant to be together, wouldn't he have told her?

Then again, she'd never told him.

He wasn't anything like the hero she'd once imagined for herself. He would probably never read Jane Austen, and he was a hell of a lot more annoying than any dream man ought to be.

But he was hers. The fact that he was in Australia didn't change that. If she had to fly halfway around the world to tell him she loved him, then that's what she'd do.

And she had the proper armor for the battle now. As she carried the dress out of the store—the employee had triple bagged it so it wouldn't get wet—Jane decided that if she brought it to Australia, there was no way Caleb could resist her.

She caught a taxi to Brooklyn, anxious to get home and plan her trip. The rain intensified during the drive, and even though she only had to make it from the cab to her apartment building, she was soaked by the time she crossed the sidewalk.

She lugged her bags inside and trudged up the stairs to the third floor.

Then she stopped cold. There was light underneath her door.

Had she left a lamp on when she left? No . . . she was almost sure she hadn't.

She'd asked a neighbor to water her plants. Maybe it was her.

But just in case it was a band of burglars, she set down her suitcase and dress bag, pulled out her phone, and got ready to dial 911 as she unlocked the door and pushed it open.

The phone slipped from her fingers and landed on the floor.

Caleb was sitting on her sofa, surrounded by folded paper cranes in every color imaginable. Pale green and dark green and indigo and mauve, periwinkle and goldenrod and primrose and lavender, scarlet and white and silver and gold.

Origami cranes, hundreds of them, covering her couch and the coffee table and the floor.

She came in slowly, staring, and Caleb rose to his feet and looked back at her, a half-finished crane in one hand.

He was wearing jeans and a red button-down shirt, and he'd shaved since the last time she'd seen him. He looked warm and sexy and good enough to eat, and she was very aware of her own sodden, bedraggled appearance.

"What are you . . ." She stopped. "I don't . . ." She stopped again.

He set the crane down and took a step toward her. "Whoever folds a thousand paper cranes will be granted one wish."

She raised her icy hands and held them to her hot cheeks. Was this really happening? Was Caleb really here?

She tried to focus on his words. One wish, he'd said.

"What will you wish for?" she asked.

"To be with you."

The fault line in her heart began to crack.

He cleared his throat. "I was hoping to finish before you got back, but it turns out a thousand cranes really is a lot. I meant to write you a letter. Something romantic, to show you I could. I was going to leave it for you. I didn't mean to be here in person. I thought you'd have some time to read the letter and think about things before you had to deal with me."

He closed the distance between them, walking carefully to avoid stepping on the cranes.

"I should go," he murmured. "You just got back, and you probably want to rest. I'll write that letter and send it to you. Then we can talk, if you want to."

Instinct made her reach for him before he could leave, and she got hold of his right arm.

At the feel of hard muscle under her hand, electricity shot through her. There was a buzzing, vibrating hum in her body and a ringing in her ears.

"Wait," she said, her voice trembling. "What was the letter going to say?"

Caleb's breath was shallow and ragged.

"I don't know," he said. "I swear to God, I can't think straight right now. You have that effect on me."

The vibration was in the air around her, connecting her to Caleb. It was like everything operated at a different frequency when he was around.

She took a deep breath, and now his scent was around her, too, like rainwater and pine sap.

"Try," she said. "Try to tell me."

"I don't know. I'm bad at this—you know I am." He swallowed. "I was going to apologize for leaving you on Prince Edward Island. Beg your forgiveness, actually. And I was going to say something about how I can't live without you." He closed his eyes. "Something about how I love you."

Her heart tightened in her chest until there was an ache behind her breastbone. She reached out with her other hand, and now she had both his arms.

"I was going to seduce you," she said.

He opened his eyes and stared down at her.

"What?"

"I was going to fly to Australia and seduce you. With this."

She let go of him and stepped out into the hall, where she'd dropped her things. She came back in with the boutique bag and pulled out the dress to show him.

He looked at it for a moment and then back at her.

"You were going to fly to Australia?"

"Yes."

"To seduce me."

"Yes."

"With that dress."

"That was my plan." She paused. "After I told you I love you."

He stepped close and slid a hand into her hair, and she shivered.

His voice was husky. "Darlin', you could seduce me in a burlap sack."

She closed her eyes. "I wanted to wear something beautiful."

He used his other hand to cup the side of her face. "You don't need it."

"But I wanted it," she whispered. "I've wanted it from the moment I saw it."

He stepped even closer, close enough that she could feel his body heat.

When he spoke, his breath tickled her ear. "Tell me what else you want."

"You. I want you. Caleb—"

But she didn't have time to say anything else.

Caleb's mouth brushed over hers in the merest breath of a kiss. Then he did it again, and again, until she felt drunk on the whispering friction of their lips. Only when she felt her whole body going soft and pliant did he move a hand to the back of her head and deepen the kiss, his tongue delving into her mouth and tangling with hers until she looped her arms around his neck and arched up into him.

He broke the kiss with a gasp.

"Hang on, Jane. Before we get carried away."

"I want to get carried away," she panted, her heart pounding.

But he led her firmly over to the couch, moving cranes so she had a place to sit beside him.

His expression was serious. "I shouldn't have kissed you. Not until we had a chance to talk."

She started to smile. "If you hadn't kissed me, I would have kissed you."

He reached out as though he couldn't help it, brushing her lips with the back of a knuckle. "Yeah, sexual chemistry isn't one of our challenges. But we do have challenges."

She nodded, her mouth tingling where he'd touched her. "I know."

"But I think we can make it work," he went on. "I want to live with you here in New York, like you talked about. I'll run the business from here, and I'll hire more people to lead expeditions so I don't have to be away from you so much."

Her heart swelled. "I don't want you to give up any expeditions. That would be like taking away your eyesight or locking you in a prison cell. I don't want that."

He shook his head. "You've got it backward. The only prison cell would be a life without you."

She caught her breath. "Caleb—"

"Ever since I started traveling, I've been looking for something spectacular. Something that would take my breath away." He paused.

"Now I've found what I was looking for. And if I lose you, it won't matter if I see all the wonders of the world, because they wouldn't mean a thing. I'd rather stay in New York with you than see the most incredible scenery on earth. Because without you to help me see the magic, that's all it would be. Scenery."

Her eyes filled with tears. "That's a pretty good speech for a guy who doesn't do speeches."

"Yeah, well, I've had some time to think about this. Did I mention how long it takes to fold a thousand paper cranes?"

She started to smile. "What made you think of doing it?"

"I remembered the cranes you made in December. And I remembered you saying you'd tried it a few times when you were a kid, but that you'd never finished." He paused. "I don't have an imagination like yours, and I'm not much good with poetry and fairy tales. But if there's one thing I'm good at, it's getting things done. I want to help you turn your dreams into reality. I want to help with your bookstore, and be here for you while you finish a book, and watch you send it off to a publisher."

She raised an eyebrow. "You've never read my writing. Maybe it's terrible."

"Maybe it isn't."

She took a breath and let it out slowly. "But what about you? I don't want you to run the business from here and let other people lead the expeditions. I want you to keep exploring. And I wouldn't mind coming along sometimes," she added. "Just not all the time."

"Okay, so, we'll compromise." He paused. "You know, I think we've had it wrong all this time. On the surface we seem so different, but who we are inside isn't different at all. Only what we do and where we do it. I explore out there, and you explore in here," he said, touching his temple.

"I like that," she said. "I like thinking we're both explorers in different ways. Maybe it won't be so hard for us to figure this out after all."

"I sure hope so." He took both her hands in his. "Because I don't want to live my life without you."

The fault line in her heart cracked wide open, and it was the sweetest pain she'd ever known.

She took a deep breath. "I feel the same way. Oh, Caleb . . . I wish I could take you back to Prince Edward Island. It was so beautiful, and everything made me think of you. I feel like we were cheated out of our time there."

"Well, then, let's get it back. Let's go there on our honeymoon."

She blinked. "There's going to be a honeymoon?"

"Hell yes."

"For there to be a honeymoon, there'd have to be a wedding."

He grinned. "I thought of that, too."

He reached into the pocket of his jeans and pulled out a ring box. He opened it, and a red stone winked at her against black velvet.

"It's a ruby," he said. "There are a lot of reasons I chose a ruby instead of a diamond, if you're interested, but . . ."

He was holding a ring.

He was proposing.

"Wait," she said. "Wait, wait, wait." Everything around her was so beautiful—the delicate paper cranes, the ring in Caleb's hand, Caleb himself.

And then there was her. "I look awful. I'm a soggy mess. I don't want you to remember me like this when you think about . . ."

"Sorry," he said. "This is exactly how I want to remember this moment, down to the last detail." He paused. "Except that you look a little cold."

"I am," she said. "Let me change, and then we can do the proposal over again."

He shook his head. "I've got a better idea for warming you up," he said, and then he was sliding the ring onto her finger and pulling her into his arms.

Her body melted into his. "I love you," she said, the words muffled against his chest.

"I love you, too," he said. "God, I love you so much."

Warmth spread through them both. And as they held each other close, heartbeat to heartbeat, Jane knew she'd never be cold again.

ACKNOWLEDGMENTS

Thanks to the amazing team at Montlake, especially Maria Gomez. Thanks to Charlotte Herscher, editor extraordinaire, for her insight. Thanks to my incredible husband, who's read every word I've ever written and is still willing to come back for more. Thanks to my son for his all-around awesomeness and for going with me to Prince Edward Island. And my deepest gratitude to Tara Gorvine, the best friend and critique partner in the world, who *always* knows what's sexy. You guys are the best.

ABOUT THE AUTHOR

Abigail Strom started writing stories at the age of seven and has never been able to stop. In addition to writing for Montlake Romance, she has written for Harlequin and is also the author of the self-published Hart University series, the first book of which earned a 2016 RITA nomination. Her books have been translated into several languages, including French, German, Italian, Spanish, Dutch, and Turkish. Abigail also writes the steamy paranormal Blood and Absinthe series under the name Chloe Hart. Learn more about the author and her work at www.abigailstrom.com and www.authorchloehart.com.

Abigail earned a BA in English from Cornell University as well as an MFA in dance from the University of Hawaii and held a wide variety of jobs—from dance teacher and choreographer to human resources manager—before becoming a full-time writer. Now she works in her pajamas and lives in New England with her family, who are incredibly supportive of the hours she spends hunched over her computer.